a Hero for Hailey

Copyright © 2020 D.E. Haggerty

All rights reserved.

D.E. Haggerty asserts the moral right to be identified as the author of this work.

ISBN: 9798691399442

A Hero for Hailey is a work of fiction. The names, characters, places, and incidents portrayed in it are the product of the author's imagination. Any resemblance to actual persons, living or dead, events or locations is entirely coincidental.

All rights reserved. No part of this publication may be reproduced, stored in a retrieval system, or transmitted, in any form or by any means, electronic, mechanical, photocopying, recording or otherwise, without the prior permission of the author.

No portion of this book may be reproduced in any form without written permission from the publisher or author, except as permitted by U.S. copyright law.

Also By D.E. Haggerty

A Protector for Phoebe
A Soldier for Suzie
A Fox for Faith
A Christmas for Chrissie
A Valentine for Valerie
A Love for Lexi
How to Date a Rockstar
How to Love a Rockstar
How to Fall For a Rockstar
How to Be a Rockstar's Girlfriend
How to Catch a Rockstar
My Forever Love
Forever For You
Just For Forever
Stay For Forever
Only Forever
Meet Disaster
Meet Not
Meet Dare
Meet Hate

Bragg's Truth
Bragg's Love
Perfect Bragg
Bragg's Match
Bragg's Christmas
About Face
At Arm's Length
Hands Off
Knee Deep
Molly's Misadventures

Chapter 1

If I never see a man wearing a panther print thong again, it will be too soon. ~ Text from Hailey to Suzie

"We have to stop meeting like this."

I roll my eyes. Corny. "Dude, if we didn't meet like this, you couldn't afford to take your girl out to fancy restaurants every weekend," I say as I slap the fifty-dollar bill in his hand.

Ralph, the motel desk clerk, sticks the money in his front pocket. "Room 234. Second floor. Half-way down. Curtains are open."

"When did they arrive?" There is a precise timing to my work.

"About ten minutes ago."

"Awesome." Ten minutes should be about the right amount of time.

I wave to Ralph as I walk out of the reception area. Motels are the best. Since all the rooms open on to a public breezeway, it makes my life easier. Much easier. You don't want to know the situations I've gotten myself into when I've had to work in hotels. When people say they pee their pants in fright, they are not kidding. Trust me. You don't want to know.

I climb the stairs and walk down the hallway toward room 234. As I do, I scan the area to make sure no one sees me. Don't get me wrong. I'm not doing anything illegal, but people tend to freak out when they see someone taking pictures of other people inside a motel room.

In my defense, it's not like I enjoy watching random people doing naughty things. Seriously, I don't. Yuck. Hairy backs, wiggly bottoms, and saggy boobs? No, thanks. When I have sex, the lights are always off. Although my boobs do not sag. I kind of wish they did. Sagging would mean I had at least some boob action going on. Spoiler alert – I don't.

But taking pictures of people having sex is my job. Well, kind of my job. I'm not exactly a photographer. Nope. I'm a private investigator. Although, considering most of my cases involve cheating husbands and lost kittens, I'm not sure I'm allowed to call myself an investigator. Whatever. It pays the bills. And – bonus – I don't have to sit inside in some boring office.

I find room 234 halfway down the building like Ralph said it was. The curtains are open and, judging from the noises coming from inside the room, I'm right on time. I grab my camera, take off the lens cap, and tiptoe to the window. Blech. I'm right on time all right.

I start clicking away. Come on, dude. I need to see your face. But his face is buried in... Well, you don't need to know where it's buried. I close my eyes for a five-count. When I open them, he lifts his head with a cocky grin on his face. Aha! Gotcha! I snap the money shot and take a few steps back straight into a brick wall.

Hold up. I know there wasn't a wall on the other side of the breezeway, which can only mean one thing. I slowly swivel around and look up. Since I'm five-foot-eight, I can look most people straight in the eyes. Not this time. Nope, I have to look up and up to see who the heck I bumped into. As soon as I see his face, I jump back like he's contagious. Shit. I am in deep shit.

"What do you think you're doing?"

Despite everything, I shiver at the sound of his voice. It's deep and sultry. Exactly the type of voice I would love to hear in my bedroom. No, wait. I don't want to hear *his* voice in my bedroom. I shake my head to rid myself of those crazy-pants thoughts.

I can't help myself from taking a second to peruse his body, though, because his body totally matches the deep and sultry voice. Yum. He's tall and muscular. I happen to know he's six-foot-three. The perfect height for me. Not as if this man is for me, but you get what I'm saying. And those muscles? He doesn't look like an over the top bodybuilder, but he's definitely strong enough to take care of business.

His hair is dark brown and curly. It practically dares me to run my hands through it to see if it's as soft as it looks. His strong jaw is covered with stubble. I love the rugged look of a man who can grow a beard but chooses not to. It's his eyes, though, they get me every time. They are a deep blue and, when he looks at you, you have the feeling he can read every single thought in your head. But, like I said, this man is not for me.

"I'm not doing a thing, Barnes," I say as I put away my camera.

His head jerks back. "How do you know my name?"

And now you know why I hate the guy. I know hating people is wrong, but come on, just this once I'm allowed. How can he not know my name? How?!

I roll my eyes as if him not remembering who I am doesn't feel like a kick in the gut. I also ignore his question. If he doesn't remember who I am, I am not enlightening him. Although his failure to recognize me every single time I run into him, makes me feel like the heartsick fool he used to call me when we were in high school.

"Well, it was nice seeing you again." I can't stop myself from goading him. I start to walk away, but he grabs my upper arm to stop me. I raise an eyebrow at him and dip my chin to his hand. He immediately drops it and takes a step back.

"Seriously. Who are you? How do we know each other?"

Is he a complete imbecile? Yeah, we live in a city of more than a million people, and it's been over a decade since high school, but it's not like we haven't run into each other on several occasions since then.

"It doesn't matter," I tell him and try to walk away again.

"Hold up. I'm a police officer." He takes out his badge and flips it open for me to see like I don't already know he's a police detective. "When I ask you a direct question, you answer me."

I snort. He's pulling the police card on me because he can't remember who I am? Lame, dude. Totally lame.

"If you don't tell me what I want to know, I'll be forced to arrest you for being a peeping tom."

I turn around and stomp my way back to him. "You know well and good I am not going to make these pictures public in any manner."

He shrugs. "I know nothing of the sort." He bends over and gets in my face. "Because I don't know who you are."

Oh no, he didn't. "You do know who I am, you freaking imbecile! But you don't remember, because, sorry to repeat myself here, you're a freaking imbecile!"

He growls. "I am an officer of the law. You can't call me an imbecile without repercussion."

"Fine!" I throw my hands in the air. "Arrest me. See if I care."

His brow wrinkles as if he can't understand what my problem is. My problem isn't hard to understand. Being teased by someone during your entire high school career and then promptly forgotten is enough to make a person go a bit cray-cray.

"Give me your name. You're going to have to tell me your name for me to book you anyway."

I stand on my tiptoes and get in his face, too angry to care about how stupid it is to aggravate a police office. "You might know me as Heartsick Hailey." I stare at him as a wait for his synapses to connect. When his pupils dilate, I nod and take a step back.

"It was not nice seeing you, Officer Barnes. Let's not do this again." I wave as I walk away. He doesn't follow. Of course, he doesn't.

Yep, my high school nickname was Heartsick Hailey. I dare you to come up with a more embarrassing nickname. Trust me. You can't. And how did this nickname come about? It's all Aiden-Mr. Perfect-Barnes' fault. I had the biggest crush ever on him. Quarterback, popular, smart. I didn't stand a chance. Not when I was a drama geek who starred in all the school plays. What can I say? Shakespeare is a god amongst men.

Needless to say, I was not subtle about my crush. Nope. I followed quarterback Aiden around like a lovesick puppy. Big brown eyes included. It wasn't long before everyone in his click was calling me Heartsick Hailey. And when the popular kids call you a name, the entire school follows. Even the senior yearbook has my nickname listed under my actual name.

The thing is, I always thought Aiden didn't like it when his friends called me Heartsick Hailey. No, my deluded teenaged self convinced herself Aiden was merely afraid to break rank from his friends. Snort. I'm such an idiot.

I rush down the stairs and practically run to my car. I know Aiden isn't following me, but I swear I can feel his eyes watching me. And I don't like the feeling. Not at all.

Chapter 2

If I had a dime for every time a man lied to his wife, bet you would stop bitching about needing my receipts. ~ Text from Hailey to Suzie

"I'm back, Suzie!" I shout when I enter the office of our little private investigation business, *You Cheat, We Eat*. Feel free to giggle at the name. I know I do. Suzie is my best friend and business partner. She's the one who runs the office while I'm off catching cheaters doing what they do best – cheat.

The offices of *You Cheat, We Eat* look exactly like you'd expect a gumshoe detective's office to look. The name of the agency is etched into the glass front door and, when you open the door, you enter a small reception area. This is Suzie's domain and she reigns supreme here.

Behind Suzie are the offices. The top half of the walls are frosted glass, the bottom half wood paneling which has seen better days, far better days. I'm the only 'detective' at the moment, but we have two additional offices. One of the offices is where the files and the copy machine are kept, while the other one is full of boxes of, I don't know what.

The offices of our PI business may be cliché, but Suzie is anything but. She's no glasses-wearing, hair in a bun, professionally clothed secretary lookalike. For starters, her red hair is short and spiky. She's also only two inches over five-foot-tall, although she does have curves I'm seriously jealous of. And last but not least, she likes to wear her food. Yep, you'll often see remnants of her last meal spilled on her clothes.

"Did you get the money shot?" Suzie asks with a waggle of her eyebrows.

Unlike me, she doesn't have a problem with pictures of people having sex. Of course, she isn't the one wading into the dirty world of cheaters to take the pictures. Talk about a disaster waiting to happen. Not only is she the klutziest person I've ever met, but the woman can't keep quiet for longer than thirty seconds. Seriously, thirty seconds. I've timed her on multiple occasions.

Suzie is the reason I ended up in the private investigator business. I had no plans to become a PI. Nope. It wasn't even on my radar. I studied drama at college, although I had no plans to rush off to Hollywood and become a movie star. As if.

I know I'm not completely unfortunate looking. To be honest, I'm kind of pretty in a fresh-faced Midwest kind of way. Brown, wavy hair and dark brown eyes. I'm lucky enough to be skinny as well, although I would kill for some curves. But the competition in Hollywood would do me in. Always having to look your best. Yuck. Most days, I'm happy if I remember to brush my hair. And never knowing who is a real friend and who's hiding a dagger behind her back? Where do I not sign up?

Instead, I planned to become a high school drama teacher. After all, I loved performing plays in high school. But there was one teensy weensy problem with my plan. Apparently, having a potty mouth is not 'good for the children'. Insert eye roll here. You grow up with a single father who owns a bar and not end up with a potty mouth. I dare you.

I was working at my dad's bar when Suzie came to me convinced her fiancé was cheating on her. Turns out, she was right. It also turned out I'm really good at finding out people's secrets. For some reason, people look at my face and see honesty. Snort. Guess those drama classes paid off after all. Before I knew it, I had an office and Suzie as a sidekick.

Lucky for me, my sidekick did study something useful in college – business management. She takes care of all the admin and finance stuff I can't begin to understand.

I hand Suzie my camera. "It's all yours. Enjoy." I sink into one of the chairs across from her desk.

She squeals before switching on the camera and starting to scroll through the pictures. "Oh my. Someone needs his back waxed. You really should take some business cards from my waxing specialist with you."

"How would that work? Excuse me, please, can you stop cheating on your wife, so I can hand you this business card? By the way, your wife is going to sue you for all you're worth when I give her these pictures."

"There's no need to get snippy. You could shove the card under the hotel room door or something." She starts to set the camera down, but she's not looking at what she's doing and nearly sets the thing down on thin air.

"Watch it," I shout and rush to the desk to stop my obnoxiously priced camera from falling to the ground and breaking into a gazillion pieces. Told you the woman is a klutz.

"Oopsie."

I don't bother responding to her klutz moment. Instead, I move onto more important matters. "I'm starving. What's for lunch?"

It's nearly three o'clock, but I haven't had time to grab anything to eat yet. I thought being a PI and chasing cheaters would mean a lot of late nights. It turns out a ton of cheaters do the dirty deed on their lunch break.

Suzie opens a drawer and starts throwing things on the desk – a bag of tortilla chips, a candy bar, a bag of popcorn.

"Stop," I tell her. "I want real food."

She stares at me as if she has no clue what real food is.

"You know, not processed stuff."

She gasps and pulls the food to her bosom. "Shush. Don't you dare insult my lovelies. You'll hurt their feelings."

"I need meat. Something I can take a bite out of."

She abandons her precious cargo to narrow her eyes on me. "What happened?"

Damn it. The woman may be klutzy and loud-mouthed, but stupid she is not. I should have taken the damn tortilla chips and moved on. "Nothing," I say and stand, intent on hiding in my office. "I have a potential client coming soon. I need to do a background check."

"You oversold it, chickadee. One, I do the background checks. And two, the client isn't coming for two hours. What happened? Don't make me repeat myself for a third time."

"What are you going to do? TP my car? Oh, I'm so scared."

This is not an example I pulled out of thin air. Suzie likes to TP the houses and cars of her enemies. I don't want to think about how much toilet paper was wasted after I told her that her fiancé was cheating on her. Good thing she has a Costco membership.

"Stop stalling. You're going to tell me eventually anyway."

Ugh! I hate when she's right. I sink back in the chair. "I ran into Aiden."

"Aiden the asshole?"

Suzie and I are friends from way back. She knows all about Heartsick Hailey. In fact, she's a front-row witness to the whole Heartsick Hailey embarrassing episode in my life.

"Did he say anything?"

I snort. "Um, no. He still doesn't remember who I am."

"How is the guy a detective? Blind people are more observant than him. Actually, that's a slur on blind people. Strike my words from the record. Anyway, what did you do?"

"I tried to take the high road."

Suzie guffaws and slaps her hand on her desk. "You? Take the high road?"

"I did. I tried to walk away."

"But you didn't."

Ugh. She knows me too well. Although I did try to walk away, I didn't manage to get further than the top of the stairs. I should have hightailed my ass out of there without letting him know I know who he is. Instead, I couldn't help myself from opening my big fat mouth.

"He knows who I am now."

"I bet he does. Did you give him a verbal tongue lashing?"

This is why working with friends doesn't work. They know you too well. I may have prepared a speech should I ever run into Mr. I-Don't-Remember-I-Tortured-You-In-High-School again. A speech I completely and totally forgot about the minute I laid my eyes upon Aiden Barnes. The man is entirely too good-looking. It's not fair.

When I keep my mouth zipped shut, Suzie tuts and reaches into her drawer to pull out a Reese's Peanut Butter cup. I'm addicted to them, as is she. Normally, she has to keep her stash under lock and key. She throws the treat at me. I catch it and practically shove it in my mouth before I can get the wrapping off.

"The speech will be even better now he knows who you are."

Yeah, right.

"Men are assholes. I don't know why you let him get to you. Let it go already. I've gotten over my hang-ups about Toby."

What a liar. She rants and raves about her cheater, cheater pumpkin eater ex whenever she's had more than one mug of beer. She's also been known to drunk dial him. I may have six inches on her but wrestling her phone from her clutches once she's made up her mind is impossible. It doesn't help she tends to stick her phone down the front of her pants whenever we start to wrestle. We may be best friends and have seen each other through thick and thin, but down her pants is the one place I am not willing to go. Nope.

Fortunately, when she's sober, she acts somewhat normal about the situation. I managed to convince her to delete Toby's contact information from her phone. I even got her to block him on social media. She can still unblock him, but I'm pretty sure her drunk ass would get distracted before she can manage the task.

I stand. "It's fine. I'm fine. No biggie."

I walk off before she can call me on my shit. How pathetic am I? Still fixated on some guy I crushed on in high school? Oh sure, I've had plenty of boyfriends since then. Well, not plenty, I'm not a slut. But, I've dated. I've even had long-term relationships. Not with any man my pops would approve of, but the man is one hard nut to crack.

And yet, every single man I've ever been with is compared to Aiden Fucking Barnes. Yep, pathetic.

Chapter 3

What does the sign on an out-of-business brothel say? Beat it. We're closed. ~ Text from Hailey to Pops

"Hi, Honey, I'm home," I shout as I walk into my dad's bar. I love Pops' bar, the McGraw's Pub. It feels like home to me. As it should, I practically grew up in the place.

The bar is exactly what you expect from a place called McGraw's Pub. There's a polished wooden bar covering one side of the room with bottles of whiskey from everywhere from Tennessee to Ireland to Japan displayed on the wall behind. There are three taps – one for the Irish pub must-have Guinness, one for the local favorite Miller Lite, and one for whatever microbrew is all the rage at the moment. Battered but well-kept wooden chairs and tables are scattered throughout the room. Along the walls are booths with bench seats in dark-green upholstery. On the brick walls hang the requisite antique advertisements for anything Irish from whiskey to corny images about cold beer and warm friends.

"Get over here and give your old dad a hug," Pops shouts from behind the bar.

Old dad. Not even close. He was barely twenty-five when I was born making him a whooping fifty-six-years old. He's what romance novelists like to call a silver fox. Maybe it sounds sick to think your dad is good-looking, but I'm being objective. Also, I'd have to be blind not to notice the number of women who come into the pub, order frou-frou drinks, and then spend the entire evening making googly eyes at my dad.

Pops hates those women. Not me. I can recognize a cash opportunity when I see one. When I was a teenager working at the bar, I bought a bunch of martini glasses to service this crowd. Not to brag or anything, but Pops now has a whole stash of frou-frou glasses from Copa de Balons for gin and tonics to Collins glasses for mojitos.

"Hi, Pops," I greet as I walk behind the bar. He enfolds me in his arms and – presto chango – every bad thing from the day disappears. His hugs are magic.

"Bad day?" he asks when I cling to him like a sock stuck to a sweater straight out of the dryer.

"Meh."

"Hey! What's this? You only got loving for your old pops? What about me?"

I smile as I release Pops. "Hey, Lenny."

Lenny waggles his brow as he leans over the bar to squeeze my shoulder. "How's it going, doll?"

I shrug. I can't lie to him. Pops' group of poker buddies can spot a lie a mile off. They take their poker and poker faces very seriously. But I'm not telling him I ran into my high school nemesis either. I'm not in high school anymore. I can deal with my problems on my own, thank you very much.

"Why are men like diapers?" Barney shouts as he walks into the bar.

I roll my eyes. Here we go. My dad's poker buddies like to one-up each other with jokes, often dirty jokes. Pops used to have a fit about them telling dirty jokes in front of me, but he gave up last year when I turned thirty. As if I was some innocent virgin who didn't take dirty pictures for a living until I hit the big 3-0 or something.

"Why?" I ask Barney.

"They're usually full of shit but thankfully disposable."

I laugh. He hit the nail on the hammer there. "Right on, brother." I bump Barney's fist as he joins our group huddled at the end of the bar.

"What's happened?" he asks. "And who do we need to kill?"

Am I so easy to read? Do I need to ask my college for a refund for all those drama classes? I need to work on my poker face.

"No, Babycakes, you don't," Pops says as he puts his arm around me and squeezes. Damn. I spoke my thoughts out loud again.

"It's no big deal. Just a long day of taking pictures of men cheating on their wives."

"Not all men are cheaters, honey." Pops is speaking from experience. He has never cheated on Mom despite her leaving him high and dry when I was twelve. We've heard neither hide nor hair of her since, but his loyalty to her remains.

Trust me, I've done everything I can to get my dad to move on. I've set him up with my friends' mothers. I tried hooking him up with single teachers in high school. Hell, I've brought random strangers into the bar to meet him. Nothing works. Nothing. The man is still in love with my mom. On the one hand, I have to admit I love how loyal he is. But Mom does not deserve his loyalty. Not one single bit.

"What's everyone whispering about?" Wally asks as he and Sid join us.

"Someone has man trouble," Sid guesses.

Pops' poker group consists of four men besides him – Lenny, Barney, Wally, and Sid. The five of them served in the same unit in the Gulf War. Pops got out after he served his five years, but the rest of them were lifers. They did their twenty years and retired around the same time Mom took off for good. They saw me through my teenage years and consider themselves my uncles. I love them. I truly do. But it's irritating as all get out, they can read me like an open book. I'm an actress for crying out loud. Well, not a paid actress, but I studied drama and graduated summa cum laude. That should count for something.

"I do not have man troubles. I'm just hungry."

Pops jumps into action. "Carol, we need a hamburger and fries stat."

Carol pops her head out of the partition between the bar and the kitchen. "Coming right up. And, Hail? And whoever he is doesn't deserve you."

I groan as I walk to the tap and pour myself a New Glarus Wisconsin Belgian Red. My dad may be annoying the hell out of me, but I can't knock the beers he chooses for the microbrew tap. I take a long drink and sigh as I set my beer down. I needed that.

Before I know what's happening, Pops is pushing me toward a table with my gang of uncles following him. This is not going to be good. I try to head them off at the pass.

"How is a girlfriend like a laxative?" When no one takes the bait, I continue. "They both irritate the shit out of you."

Barney gives me a high-five, but the others shake their heads with frowns on their faces. If an inappropriate joke can't put a smile on their faces, I'm in trouble.

Carol plops a plate overflowing with fries down on the table, along with a smaller plate with a hamburger. "You need to get some meat on your bones," she complains as she walks away.

Meat on my bones? Not going to happen. I'm one of those women who other women hate because I can eat whatever I want and not gain a pound. Of course, I also don't have any boobs to speak of and my behind is as flat as an English lager. Apparently, the English don't like head. Guess I won't be dating an English man anytime soon then.

I bite into the burger and groan. I wasn't lying. I'm starving. I never did get around to eating lunch after Suzie called me on my shit about Aiden. I look up and five sets of eyes are watching my every move. I cough and have to take a gulp of my beer before I choke.

"Are you guys planning to stare at me the entire time I eat?"

"It's the only way we can make sure you're eating," Sid answers as if his answer is completely normal. It isn't. I'm thirty-one. I can take care of myself.

Pops waits until I finish every last fry. Then, he stacks my plates on the next table and gives me the dad stare. You know the one – it makes you feel guilty even though seconds before you were convinced you were in the right.

I throw my hands in the air. "Fine! What do you want to know?"

"I want to know why you had the droopy face when I walked in," demands Sid.

I do not have a droopy face. I could argue with them. Say I have no idea what they're talking about or claim they're making a big deal out of nothing, but it would be a complete and total waste of breath.

"I ran into someone from high school today."

It suddenly sounds like a thunderstorm has arrived in the bar with all the growling the uncles are doing. Geez. Talk about overreacting.

"It's not a big deal."

"If it weren't a big deal, you wouldn't have the droopy face," Pops says as he reaches over and massages my neck.

"Those high school boys were assholes to you. I couldn't kick their asses then, but I sure as hell can and will now. Give me a name," Lenny demands.

"I think not." I shake my head. "He's a cop. I don't have enough bail money."

"You think I'd get caught?" Lenny frowns. "Where's the love?"

"I know you would get caught." The word subtle is not in Lenny's vocabulary.

"I'll go with him," Wally offers. Now, there's a disaster waiting to happen. Wally is sneaky. He's also secretive. I'm fairly certain he continued working for the government in a black ops kind of situation after he retired from the Army. I tried doing a background check on him once and it came up completely empty. If that doesn't spell up to no good, I don't know what does.

"I am not spending my Saturdays visiting my uncles in prison after they're convicted of murder. You know what they do to cop-killers in prison, don't you?"

Pops has had enough. "Tell me what happened," he demands in the no-nonsense voice he reserves for when his patience is running thin.

I shrug. "Nothing happened. Like I've been saying." I pause and look around the table. Judging by the raised brows, no one is buying the shit I'm shoveling. "Fine. He didn't recognize me."

"Oh, Babycakes." Pops folds me into his arms while the rest of them pat me on the shoulder. "If he didn't recognize what a beautiful, wonderful woman you are, he isn't worth your time."

"Don't I know it," I mutter and almost believe myself.

I can practically feel the tension leak out of my uncles. Thank goodness. The angry vibe in the air was giving me a headache.

"Who's ready for me to kick their ass in pool?" Barney asks.

I giggle. "I bet you ten bucks I can run the table before you can pick up your cue."

I'm full of it. Barney practically lives in the bar. If he's not sitting around talking shit with his buddies, he's playing pool. I don't stand a chance, and I don't care.

Chapter 4

If you wanted me to hire a cleaner, you could have said so. ~ Text from Suzie to Hailey

I'M SURPRISED TO find the offices to *You Cheat, We Eat* locked the next morning. Suzie is usually at her desk long before I arrive on the scene. Unlike Ms. Cheery, I am not a morning person. I tend to saunter into the office after nine. But Suzie is always at her desk at 8 o'clock on the dot. I check my watch. Huh. It's not even eight yet. This has to be a personal record, but no way was I spending another minute in bed tossing and turning trying not to think about a certain handsome but annoying detective.

I unlock the door and push it open before flicking on the lights. When my eyes catch sight of the room, I start backing up. Shit. Shit. Shit. What the hell happened here? The place is a freaking disaster. There are papers strewn every freaking where. Not an inch of bare space is to be seen. Suzie is going to be pissed. But, first things first, I pull out my phone and call the non-emergency number for the police department to report a burglary.

You'd think as a private investigator I'd have some 'contact' on the force, but that's bullshit made up by the movies. Besides, I don't have much of a need for the police. I investigate cheating spouses and insurance claims. You know the claims I'm talking about. When a worker says he was injured on the job and can't work anymore, but in reality, the guy is running marathons. Not stuff the police usually get involved in. Although it is technically fraud, most insurance companies don't pursue it as such. They're just happy not to have to part with their precious cash.

Once I get off the phone with the police, I text Suzie to tell her there's no rush this morning. I don't mention the burglary, but the woman has been my best friend since grade school. She can read between the lines.

Do I need to get donuts for the coppers?

See what I mean? I don't bother responding. She'll do what she wants to anyway. Besides, I could totally go for a cinnamon twist.

I haven't been waiting in the hall long before two uniformed police officers come rushing out of the elevator with their weapons drawn. Overreact much? I wave and point to my offices.

The duo races into my offices. I don't follow. I know better. I may not work with the police often, but I did take some police procedure classes when I decided to become a private investigator. Although you can get licensed without taking any classes, you only need to pass a licensing exam, I thought it would be helpful to take a few classes before sitting for the exam and starting my business.

I hear shouts of "Clear!" before the police officers return. Thank my lucky stars, their weapons are now holstered.

"These your offices?"

Before I get a chance to answer, the elevator doors open again. I glance over, expecting to see Suzie arrive with some coffee and donuts. Instead, my eyes fall upon the one person in the entire city I do not want to see. You guessed it – Aiden Barnes. Twice in two days. Guess my stars aren't lucky after all.

Unlike my calm, cool, and collected head, my body lights up like a Christmas Tree at the sight of the hunky detective. My body doesn't care he doesn't remember who we are or about how he humiliated us in high school. Nope, the hussy is all hot and bothered for the man.

"Detective Barnes." There. I didn't sound like a lovesick fool. Go me.

"Hailey McGraw." Aw, someone did his homework. Aren't we impressed? Nope. Big whoop-de-doo.

"You want to tell me what happened here?" He motions to my offices. His eyes widen and his lips tip up when he catches sight of the name of my firm. People either think the name, *You Cheat, We Eat,* is hilarious or – if they're my dad – think it's demeaning.

I shrug. "Not sure. I arrived about fifteen minutes ago to this mess. I called the police. End of story."

"And the door was locked when you arrived?"

"Of—" I stop. "Now I'm thinking about it, only the doorknob lock was engaged. The deadbolt wasn't."

"Which means someone definitely broke into your office."

What did he think? I came in here and made a giant mess and then called the police. I open my mouth, intent on telling him exactly what breed of idiot I think he is, but the elevator dings and Suzie walks out. She's carrying a huge box of donuts and a carton of coffees. Yes! Coffee! Give me all the coffee. As she rushes to us, she stumbles and seems to trip on air. She starts to go down. Oh shit, the coffee. Before I can move, Aiden is there steadying her arm.

"Thanks, Aiden." Her eyes dilate in interest as she looks him up and down.

He smiles at her. A full-blown smile. "Any time, darling."

A pit of acid churns in my stomach. What the hell? Who is he calling darling? Wait. Stop. I refuse to be jealous. I will not demean myself by being jealous of a man I do not want smiling at my best friend. Nope. I refuse.

"You got a cinnamon twist in there for me?" I ask to stop the weird thoughts churning in my head.

Suzie steps back from Aiden and rolls her eyes at me. "No, of course not. How could I know you wanted a cinnamon twist when it's the only donut you ever eat? Here." She hands me the box of donuts.

I pull out a twist and grab a coffee. I take a large gulp before tearing off a piece of cinnamon goodness and shoving it into my mouth. Yum. Just what the doctor ordered.

My moment of tranquility is ruined when she screams, "What the hell happened here? I am not cleaning this up. Whoever made this mess can get their ass back in here and clean it up."

"Sure, Suze. I'll get right on finding the burglar, so he can return and clean up his mess."

"Speaking of the burglary." Aiden clears his throat. "Is there anything missing?"

"How would I know? I saw the mess and called you guys."

Suzie snorts. "As if she'd know if anything's missing anyway. Organized is not in her vocabulary."

"At least I'm not an obsessive-compulsive cleaner," I retort. And I am not kidding. The woman is a complete and utter clean freak. I had to ban her from cleaning my office because the overwhelming smell of cleaning fluids made me sick to my stomach. Lemony fresh scent, my ass.

Before we get a chance to get into a smackdown fight, something we've been known to do in the past, Aiden steps in between us. "Maybe Suzie can have a look inside to see if anything's missing while I ask you some questions?" he asks but his tone of voice clearly says he expects his orders to be followed. I roll my eyes before motioning to Suzie to go ahead inside.

"Who wants donuts?" she shouts as she walks into the offices.

"What do you want to know?" I ask once I've watched Suzie successfully maneuver through the office without causing any chaos. Although, considering the state of the office, I'm not sure how she'd manage to cause more chaos.

"Who would do this?"

I shrug. "No idea."

He raises an eyebrow and stares me down. Am I supposed to be intimidated? "Dude, you've seen me in action. Or have you forgotten about that too? It was only yesterday." I don't give him a chance to defend himself before I continue. "Look. I investigate cheaters." I point to the front door. "Thus, the name of the business. There's no reason for a cheating spouse to ransack my office."

"No? You don't think the guy you were photographing yesterday wouldn't want to make sure those photographs never reach his wife?"

"Dude, the guy yesterday had no clue I was there. They never do. They're preoccupied when I take my pics. There's a reason it's called 'getting busy'."

He chuckles. "Yeah, but you can't be sure every single guy you've ever photographed didn't notice you."

I wrinkle my nose. "Don't you think they would have come after me right away, then? And not waited to ransack my office? How would they even know who I am? It's not like I wear a t-shirt advertising my business." This is not a random remark on my part. Suzie has seriously pushed me to get matching t-shirts for us to wear to work. Not happening.

"Regardless, whatever happened here was not random." His arm sweeps out to indicate the chaos in the office.

Well, shit. He's right. My shoulders slump. Damn. Did some idiot cheater ransack my office because he was pissed he got caught? Men are idiots.

"I need new locks."

"Yeah." He nods. "You sure do."

There goes my bottom line. Don't get me wrong. I'm not destitute, but the reason I'm not destitute is because I keep my costs to a bare minimum. Getting new locks installed is going to cost me.

"I can help you install the locks. In fact, I can meet you tonight at the hardware store and help you pick out what you need. Then, we can come back here, and I'll get them installed. Shouldn't take more than an hour."

My mouth drops open. Is he serious? He wants to help me? I lift my hand to check his temperature before I realize we don't know each other well enough for me to touch him. He grabs my hand before it drops to my side. His thumb rubs circles into my skin and I feel warmth move from that one small spot and travel all over my body. Damn. The man can pull reactions from my body without making an effort.

"I want to help, Hailey. To make up for …" he trails off with a shrug.

Oh no, he didn't. I rip my hand away from his touch. "You are not going to help me because you're sorry for being a supreme asshole in high school. I'll have Pops or one of my uncles help." In fact, Wally is probably the person to ask. He still works in security after all. Or at least, I think he does. The man is a mystery.

Aiden raises his hands and takes a step back. "I was only trying to be nice."

The patrol officers join us and for the next thirty minutes I answer questions and fill out forms. As we're finishing up, Suzie joins us.

"It doesn't look like anything was taken," she announces before shoving a donut into her mouth. Well, she tries to shove a donut in her mouth. She actually misses her mouth and nearly takes her eye out. There's chocolate glaze all over her forehead and in her hair. How is it possible to miss your mouth? Thirty-one-years of practice wasn't enough for her?

After I finish giggling at Suzie's latest antics, I address Aiden. "Since nothing is missing, can we skip reporting this whole incident? It looks like this was a waste of your time. Sorry."

Aiden grabs my hand and pulls me away from the group. My hand tingles at the contact. Stupid hand. Stupid crush. Ugh. Everything's stupid.

"You should report this. You don't know what's going on. This could be personal. Someone could be after you. Stalking you, for all you know."

I yank my hand away. "You're crazy. No one's after me. This was probably a mistake."

He opens his mouth to argue, but his phone rings. "Shit. I need to go." I start walking away. Confident I've won my argument. "Think about what I said. I need you safe."

Need me safe? Yeah, right. I wave and walk off to tell the patrol officers I'm not filing a complaint.

Chapter 5

I don't get the whole ménage à trois thing. It's like a jigsaw puzzle, but there are too many parts. ~ Text from Hailey to Suzie

THE INTERCOM CRACKLES BEFORE I hear Suzie's voice. "Ms. McGraw. Mrs. Smith is here to see you."

I groan. Not this again. Mrs. Smith – not her real name obviously – is a repeat customer, but each time she comes in I have to 'pretend' I don't know her. This is not how I expected to use the skills learned in drama school. "Send her in."

I stand and walk out from behind my desk to greet my 'new' client. The door flies open and in walks drama. Trust me, I'm an expert. I know.

Mrs. Smith sashays into the room. She is one sexy woman. She's wearing a skintight red dress showing off all her curves. She's showing so much cleavage I wouldn't be surprised if there was a nipple-gate incident. Her long, blonde hair cascades down her back. Not a hair out of place. On her face are over-sized dark sunglasses. She's also wearing a large hat.

She rips off her sunglasses. "Oh, Ms. McGraw. It's terrible. I think my husband is cheating on me." She sniffs and pats her dry eyes.

I show her to a chair. "Please, call me Hailey."

"Hailey." She grabs my hand and holds on tight. "I can't believe John would do this to me."

Yeah, yeah, I can't believe it either. Really, I can't. Because it's not true. 'John' and 'Judy' 'Smith' love each other a lot. Like, a lot a lot. Trust me, I've seen the proof. Anyway, on with the charade.

"Why do you think he's cheating?"

"Well, it's been a week since he made love to me. A week!" She opens her clutch and pulls out a handkerchief, which she places in front of her face. She doesn't touch her face. Oh no, she can't ruin her perfect make-up.

"Have you seen him with another woman?"

"N-n-n-ooo."

"Has he snuck off into another room when he gets a call?"

"I don't think so."

"Okay." I lean against my desk and drum my fingers against my thigh. "Has he been taking unexplained business trips?"

"John doesn't travel for business."

"Any unexplained meetings?"

She gasps. "Well, now you mention it, I did see he has an appointment at the Grand Hotel this afternoon at 2 p.m."

"A hotel?" I place a hand on my chest and shake my head. "This doesn't sound good, Mrs. Smith."

"I know, Hailey. It's why I came to you. I know you're the best in the business."

Now, she's pushing it. She doesn't think I'm the best in the business, but she does know I'm the one detective agency in town willing to play her game month after month. Although, considering the money she pays me, I don't know why other PI's don't jump on this business.

"Tell you what I'll do. I'll go to the hotel this afternoon. Have a peek around. And I'll let you know if he meets anyone. Okay?" She nods. "But, under no circumstance, should you go to the hotel. You hear me? You'll only make the situation worse for yourself."

She bobs her head. "Oh, I know. I won't. I don't want to see…" She gulps. "Well, you know."

Yes, I know. I also know she's a big fat liar pants. I escort her to the door with promises to do my best and keep in touch. Blah. Blah. Blah.

As soon as the door shuts behind her, I point a finger at Suzie. "No. Wait. Wait until you hear the elevator doors close." The elevator dings to announce its arrival. Suzie snorts. "Five more seconds."

The elevator doors slide shut, and Suzie bursts out laughing. "Did you … did you see today's outfit?"

"How could I not? I thought she was going to take her eye out with her own boobs."

"The sunglasses were a nice touch as well. Very Audrey Hepburn à la Breakfast at Tiffany's."

I collapse into the chair in front of her desk. "It's easy for you to laugh about it. You don't have to go to the hotel this afternoon."

Suzie reaches across her desk and pats my hand. "Poor you. You have to watch people have a threesome. Oh, boo hoo."

I snarl at her before standing and returning to my office. I need to text John Smith and make sure he's all set up to get caught with his 'lover' this afternoon.

At a quarter to two, I'm at the Grand Hotel. I walk to the reception desk where I know Mr. Smith has left an extra room key for me. The receptionist sees me coming and starts giggling.

"I love Smith days!" Peggy, the receptionist, announces as she hands me the key to room 550.

"Doesn't the drama bother your other customers?"

She waves my concern away with a flick of her hand. "Please. It's 2 p.m. Our guests are either attending boring business meetings, doing tourist junk, or they're enjoying a bit of chitty chitty bang bang themselves. Besides, Mr. Smith always pays extra for a corner room." She winks and I know the 'extra' is going straight into her pocket.

I grab the key card. "Mrs. Smith will be arriving at five after."

"I know the drill."

I walk to the bar and have a seat at the counter to wait. According to Mr. Smith, I'm more than welcome to watch the opening act, but watching is not my thing. Not at all. I'll wait until two on the dot before I make my way to the room. Andy, the bartender, sets a shot of tequila in front of me.

"Happy Smith day," he says and nods to the drink.

I smile in thanks before grabbing the glass and taking the shot.

"I think it's kind of romantic. They've been married for decades. Yet, they find a way to keep the excitement in their sex life."

I snort. Only a man would think this set-up is romantic. I knock on the counter. "Thanks for the drink."

I prepare my camera as I ride the elevator. When the elevator opens on the fifth floor, I sigh in relief to see the hallway's empty. Mrs. Smith has been known to arrive early. She gets cranky when I'm not here ahead of her.

As I walk to the end of the hallway, the noises become louder. Oh, goodie. They left the door open for me today. Sometimes, Mr. Smith likes me to bang on the door. Other times, he wants me to sneak in and take pictures. Guess I'll be sneaking in today.

The opening act is getting started when I walk in, making sure to leave the door wide open for Mrs. Smith. There's a bottle of champagne and two glasses on a side table, but they haven't been touched. The champagne is for when the main event gets started. On the bed, Mr. Smith and some random blonde are rolling around. She's still wearing her bra and panties. I glance around and notice her clothes are folded neatly on the chair closest to the door. Someone's prepared for a quick exit.

I've finished taking a few pictures when I hear a loud gasp. "John! How could you do this to me?"

I swivel and snap a picture of Mrs. Smith with her hand over her heart. Her chest is rising and falling at a rapid pace, and her eyes are dilated. I'm surprised she's not licking her lips.

John jumps out of the bed. "It doesn't mean anything, Judy. She's just some random chick I picked up."

The random chick in question grunts. "You mean this didn't mean anything to you? You said you loved me." Her voice is flat like she's reading from a script, probably because she is reading from a script. But come on, she could have put a little verve in her voice. It looked like she was enjoying the rolling around on the bed well enough.

John ignores his hook-up and approaches Judy. "I'm sorry, baby. You're the one I want." He doesn't sound like he's reading from a script.

"But." Judy sniffles. "Why…" She gestures toward the bed.

He pulls her into his arms. "It's you I want. Only you." He smashes her lips to hers and it's on like bangy kong.

As the 'mistress' passes me, I gesture to the envelope next to her clothes. She nods with a roll of her eyes. I hear her quickly dress and retreat.

Time for the main attraction. I snap away as John and Judy fall to the bed and tear each other's clothes off. I continue to take pictures as they enjoy each other. Andy the bartender was right. It is kind of romantic.

I'm not watching the entire show, though. No way. I've learned from my mistakes. Once John's manhood is visible, I'm out of here. Those are my rules and I'm sticking to them. John can offer me as much money as he wants – and he has offered me a ton of money – I'm not changing my mind. And I'm certainly not joining them. Not my thing. And, lucky for me, today is not a threesome day.

When Judy reaches for John's tighty whities, I'm out of here. I grab the envelope full of cash Judy left for me and shut the door on my way out. I know they wouldn't mind if I left the door open. Hello! Exhibitionists. But I worry about their safety. Exhibitionism is fine. Not my thing, but fine for them. But anyone could stroll off the street and walk straight into their room.

"Leaving so soon?" Peggy asks when I return the room key to her.

She giggles when I don't respond. She knows John has pressured me to join them on multiple occasions in the past. She thinks it's hilarious.

"You want to join them? I can arrange it."

Her nose wrinkles. "Ew. Gross. Old man sex."

"But good enough for me?" She's the middle-aged woman in this scenario, not me.

The phone rings. "Get out of here. I have work to do."

Likely excuse. I throw her a wave and walk out of the hotel.

Chapter 6

What did the banana say to the vibrator? Why are you shaking? She's gonna eat me! ~ Text from Hailey to Pops

I LAY MY HEAD down on the bar and groan. A pint of beer lands in front of my face. I lift my face to take a sip before laying my head back down again.

"It's a Smith day," Pops yells behind him.

"Fried cheese curds coming up," Carol responds.

"I didn't say a word," I mumble.

Pops lays a hand on my shoulder and squeezes. "You didn't have to, Babycakes. I think I know my baby girl."

He leaves to go help a customer. Good. I might tell dirty jokes to my dad, but I'm not comfortable talking about sex with him. I know he feels the same. He had to give me the sex talk when I was twelve and walked in on two people playing hide Pedro in the stockroom. I ran into the bar screaming *Pedro's missing. We need to find Pedro.*

I have never seen Pops' face redder than when he sat me down in the office and explained why we could call off the search party for Pedro. We haven't discussed the birds and the bees since, and I plan to keep it that way.

Pops returns with a basket of fried cheese curds. I pop one in my mouth before I remember. "Ouch. Hot. Burn." I take a slug of beer and sigh in relief.

"You're thirty-one years old and yet you forget to wait for the cheese curds to cool off every single time." He shakes his head. "It's like watching Suzie try to walk in high heels. You know it's going to be a disaster and yet you can't look away."

"Shaddup." I slap his arm. "I'm hungry."

He snorts. "You're always hungry. Drove me to the brink of bankruptcy when you were a teenager."

"And yet, you love me." I grin – my teeth covered in gooey cheese goodness – before I swallow the cheese curd I'm chewing on.

Pops grunts before putting his elbows on the bar and leaning forward. "By the way, you have company."

"Company?" I find a ton of clients at the bar. Pops brags about my business and before you know it, another wronged wife is sitting in a bar where she doesn't belong begging me to find out who her husband is schlepping.

Pops points to a booth in the corner. Definitely not a client. Aiden is sitting there surrounded by my uncles. I hope they're giving him a hard time.

"Did he ask to see me?" Pops nods, and I groan. Yippee. He can wait. I'm not ruining the deliciousness of fried cheese curds with his presence.

"I don't like him." He doesn't like any guys who come sniffing around me.

"Don't worry. He's not here to woo me. He probably wants to talk about the break-in at my office." The words are out before I realize my mistake. I may have accidentally on purpose neglected to tell Pops about the break-in. Oops.

"What break-in?"

"It was nothing. Nothing was stolen. Probably some dude angry he got caught with his dick out."

"And I already got her set up with a new set of locks and an alarm system," Wally says as he joins us.

Pops turns on his friend. "You knew about this and didn't tell me?"

He shrugs. "I thought Hails told you."

Pops' head looks like it's about to explode. Time to make my exit. "Sorry. I need to go deal with the detective. Maybe he has a lead."

As soon as I walk to the booth, Sid, Lenny, and Barney retreat. They grin at me before doing the whole I'm-watching-you-motion to Aiden. To his credit, Aiden doesn't shake in his boots but nods in response. Of course, he nods. What am I thinking? He's not here for any romantic reason. No. He's here to discuss my case. Duh.

"Hey, Hails," Barney says as he walks away. "How do you make a pool table laugh?" He doesn't wait for my guess before he answers, "Tickle its balls."

"Lame, Barney. Lame!"

"Hey, Detective," I say as I scooch into the booth. "Did you find anything out about who may have ransacked my office?"

"No, the case is ongoing."

"Ongoing?" I roll my eyes. "In other words, you're waiting for a clue to walk up and slap you in the face."

He chuckles. "Never heard it been put like that before."

"Then, what's up? Why are you here? I assume it's not for a beer. Pops said you wanted to see me."

I will kill Pops. Kill him dead. If he recognized Aiden and decided it was time for me to confront my high school bully.

"Yeah, yeah, I did." He clears his throat. "Actually, I have something to show you."

I lean away from him. "Dude, I'm sure it's impressive and all, but I'll pass."

He grins. "I never knew you were funny. You weren't funny in high school."

The smile dies on my face. How the hell would he know what I was like in high school? When he wasn't teasing me back then, he was avoiding me like the plague. I start scooching my way back out of the booth. "Maybe you should leave."

"Wait." He grabs my arm and stops me. I almost jump when a current of electricity flows between us. The hairs on my arms stand up and I tingle in all the right places. Damn it. Not all the right places. Not when we're talking about Aiden freaking Barnes.

He yanks his hand away. He stares at his hand as if he felt the current between us, too. But he couldn't have, could he?

He clears his throat. "Please stay. I do have something to show you."

I stare at him for a long moment with a frown on my face. I know I should act like an adult and let bygones be bygones and all, but it's not like I can suddenly stop being angry at him. "Fine, then."

I turn to shout at Pops to bring me another beer, but he's standing right in front of me already. "Thought you might be thirsty," he says as he plops two beers down on the table. He glares at Aiden for a good thirty seconds before grunting and retreating.

I pull the beer toward me. I take a sip and think *fuck it* and chug half of it. "I'm waiting. What do you have to show me?" I try to sound aloof, but I'm dying of curiosity over here.

He reaches down to the seat next to him and brings up a book. And not just any book either. Nope. It's our senior yearbook. Oh, goody. As if I haven't been reminded of my disastrous high school years enough in the past week.

"I want to show you something." He waits for me to respond but I'm done talking. He flips through the pages until he lands on the page with pictures of seniors starting with the letter M. And right there in the middle of the page is me – Hailey "Heartsick" McGraw.

Aiden taps the picture. "You're mad at me for not remembering you. But I do remember you. I just didn't recognize you."

Damn it. He has a good argument. Unlike most kids who are freed from their braces in junior high, I had braces until my first year of college. I also wore glasses, which – thanks to the miracle of laser surgery – I no longer wear. And then there's the hair. Oh, the hair. I had no idea how to tame my out of control hair back then. It wasn't until a tutor at college pulled me aside and introduced me to the miracle of hair products that I learned how to conquer my curls.

"Although I gotta say, I miss the hair."

Insert eye roll. He misses the hair? No one misses the mess my hair used to be. Least of all me. Combing the tangles out of my mass of curls was torture every single day of high school. I am not going back there.

"I'm sorry I didn't recognize you. I guess I didn't expect the drama-obsessed teenager to turn into a take-no-prisoners PI." He clears his throat. "Can we start over?"

He doesn't get it, does he? Even if I can admit there's a pretty good reason he didn't recognize me, there's another perfectly good reason I'm not ready to be his best friend. Did he forget he bullied me all through high school?

I cross my arms over my chest and lean against the back of the booth. "Have you forgotten the rest?" He looks confused. Being the generous person I am, I fill him in. "How you teased and tortured me all throughout high school?"

He shakes his head. "No, not me. It was my friends."

"Lame. Sorry, officer, peer pressure made me be an asshole."

His cheeks catch fire. "I admit I should have said something to them. I did try to protect you."

Snort. Yeah, right.

"No, really. I did. Whenever I saw you in the hallway, I'd turn around before anyone could see you."

My eyes widen. He wasn't avoiding me? He was protecting me? Yeah, no. I'm not ready to drink the Kool-Aid.

"What if I can prove it to you?"

"Prove what? I'm wrong? That every single memory I have of you laughing at me is false? What are you going to do? Give me a lobotomy? I gotta say. I am not on board with that idea."

He chuckles. "Cute and funny."

"Whatever." I start to stand. "Are we done here?"

"Wait!" He reaches for my arm, but I pull it away before he can touch me. I don't need another jolt of electricity from his touch running through me. I'm also a big fat liar, but that's a topic for another time.

"I'm serious. Let me take you out to dinner and I can prove it."

"Not gonna happen." As I walk away, I'm joined by my uncles who are glaring at Aiden. To his credit, Aiden doesn't piss his pants. He stands and throws some money on the table before nodding at the uncles as he passes.

He reaches the door but before he leaves, he shouts for all to hear, "This isn't over."

He walks outside before I have a chance to correct him. This is over. Hell, it never began. My body is not happy with my decision, but she can take a flying leap or adjust. Her choice.

Chapter 7

Why are men called male sluts? Aren't they just sluts, too? ~ Text from Suzie to Hailey

WHEN THE ELEVATOR DOORS open to the floor where the offices to *You Cheat, We Eat* are located, I can barely get out of the elevator as the hallway is completely and totally packed with people. What the hell is going on? We have interviews this morning. Our candidates aren't going to be able to get through the stupid hallway. This is a disaster.

I start pushing my way through the crowd. "No butting in line, doll," someone says and snaps her gum before moving to block my progress.

I'm late and I haven't had my coffee yet. She needs to get out of my way – now. "I'm not butting in line. I'm trying to get to work."

"Yeah, sure, doll. End of the line."

My sleepy mind catches up. Oh, shit. Are all these people here to interview with us? My eyes sweep through the crowd of people. All women who are scantily dressed. And scantily dressed is putting it nicely. Provocatively is more like it. What the hell did Suzie put in the job description?

I start pushing my way through the throng once again. The woman who yelled at me for butting in line grabs my arm to prevent my progress. I glare down at her. "Get your hands off of me."

"The end of the line is the other way."

I get in her face. "Since I own the business, I don't think I need to get in line. Now, get your hands off of me." She drops her hand. "And get out of here. We won't be hiring you."

Her face falls. "But—"

I raise my hand. "Save it. You're not who we're looking for." In fact, most of the women standing in this hallway are not what we're looking for. Freaking Suzie. What was she thinking?

I watch until the woman turns around and leaves before making my way through the rest of the hallway. The crowd parts for me since they heard me shout down the place about me doing the hiring. I open the door to the office and then slam it shut and lean against it as if the horde was trying to barge in. They aren't. Yet.

Suzie looks up from her desk with a huge smile on her face. "Did you see how many candidates we have? Way more than last time." She frowns. "I don't think I bought enough donuts."

"What do you put in the ad?"

She shrugs as her cheeks turn a dusty shade. "Just that we're looking for help."

"Your exact words."

"Um." She bites her lip. "I don't remember."

I raise my eyebrows and cross my arms over my chest. Doesn't remember, my ass.

"Looking for honey to add to our honeypot," she mutters.

I pretend to clean out my ear. I could not have heard her correctly. "You put those words in the ad? No wonder the hallway is full of hookers!"

"Hookers?" Suzie claps. "I've never met a working woman before. This is fascinating."

I stomp over to her desk, place my hands on it, and bend over to glare at her. "No, this is not fascinating. This is a disaster is what it is."

"Come on. You have to admit a hooker is the perfect person for a honey trap."

"Um, no. I don't have to admit anything of the sort. The husbands of our clients are not going to pick up a hooker at an upscale bar."

Suzie snorts. "Sure, they are. Men are pigs."

I raise my eyes to the ceiling and beg whoever's up there for a bit of patience. I get why she's a man-hater. Her ex, Toby, did her wrong in all the ways a woman can be done wrong. But she's letting it affect her work, which I can't let happen.

Running honeypot schemes is one of our main sources of income. Unfortunately, the woman who used to serve as the honey in our schemes recently got engaged. Her fiancé put the kibosh on her picking up men in bars. Even though Renee didn't actually do anything beyond a bit of flirting with the men, her man put his foot down. Which is why we're now trying to find a new Renee.

"If you'd let me play the sexpot, we wouldn't have to interview anyone."

I bite my tongue from laughing out loud at Suzie. Suzie a sexpot? Sure, the woman is cute as a button. She's also short and tends to trip on thin air when walking in heels.

"Somehow I can't imagine you flirting with men in a bar." She doesn't flirt. Not anymore at least. Seeing as how she believes all men are evil incarnate.

She sticks her bottom lip out and pouts. "I can act."

I don't bother to contradict her. This conversation is a waste of my time. She knows damn well and good I won't be using her in any honey pot scheme. She'd start lecturing the man about being faithful and ruin the operation before it could get started.

There's a knock on the door. Great, the natives are getting restless. I open the door, intent on telling everyone to go home, but the woman on the opposite side of the door stops me in my tracks. This woman is no woman of the night.

"Can I help you?"

"Um." She bites her lip. "Are you starting the interviews soon? I don't mean to rush you, but I need to feed the meter if this is going to take more time." She looks down the hallway.

I usher her in. "Come on. Let's do your interview first."

I hear grumbling in the hallway. I stick my head out and glare at the women bitching and complaining – the glare I learned from my overprotective Uncle Lenny. They immediately shut up. Works every time.

I show the woman into my office. "I'm Hailey McGraw." I stick my hand out. "Nice to meet you."

"Phoebe Ab— er Adams. Sorry, I'm nervous."

Suzie joins us. She shoves the box of donuts at Phoebe. "Donut?"

Phoebe's upper lip curls in disgust for a flash before the look is gone. "No, thank you."

Suzie hands me a cinnamon twist before taking a seat next to Phoebe. "Are you a lady of the night?"

Phoebe blinks a few times before clearing her throat. "Pardon?"

"Just checking."

"Ignore her," I say. "We usually don't let her out of her cage during the day."

I take a moment to study the woman. There's no denying she's gorgeous. Green eyes with a slight outward slant in a heart-shaped face. Plush lips that will have men eating out of the palm of her hand. Blonde hair cascading down her back with not one hair out of place.

She's wearing a wrap-around dress that hugs her hourglass figure. On her feet are a pair of sky-high heels and when her leg bounces, I can see the tell-tale red soles indicating she's wearing Louboutins. What in the hell is she doing here if she can afford five-hundred-dollar shoes?

"Do you know what we're interviewing for?" I ask because she does not look like a woman who needs a job.

"Um, yes. I think I do. I believe a honey trap is when a man or woman, woman in this case, attempts to seduce a married man who the wife, your client, believes is having an affair. Have I got it right?"

I nod. She summed it up pretty well. It's not rocket science after all.

"I gotta ask. What are you doing here?" Suzie's finger circles Phoebe and her attire. "Dressed like you are. Wearing Louboutins and is your dress an original Furstenberg?"

Phoebe's cheeks turn a lovely shade of pink. "Yes?"

"Obviously, you don't need to work for the money."

Phoebe clears her throat. "Actually, I'm starting over. I um do need a job." She pleads with me. "I have no skills, but I'm a fast learner."

And now I'm intrigued. Phoebe is a woman of mystery and I always did love a mystery. Obviously.

"Flirt with me," Suzie demands.

I slap her arm. "Stop it."

"What?" She widens her eyes as if she's some innocent. Not hardly. "You told me I couldn't be the sexpot because I don't flirt, so she needs to be able to flirt."

"I'm sorry," I tell Phoebe. "I promise she's harmless."

Phoebe learns forward and bends over slightly baring the tiniest hint of cleavage. Her eyes flutter as she says in a soft voice with a tinge of some accent I can't quite place, "It's fine, darling. I don't mind."

"She's hired!" Suzie says as she waves a hand in front of her face.

Phoebe straightens in her chair and looks at me. I nod. Of course, she's hired. She's the perfect sexpot for our honeypot.

"The pay isn't great, though. I can't tell you exactly how much as it depends on the client, but it's usually a few hundred."

"Is there…" She pauses before starting again. "Is there perhaps other work you might have I could do as well?"

Suzie answers before I get a chance. "Actually, we have a ton of filing to do due to some unexpected jerk ransacking our place the other day." She looks at me. "We can pay her out of the contingency fund."

I don't like the idea of using our emergency fund, but when I look at Phoebe, I change my mind. She has such a look of hope on her face. I can't disappoint her. I pray I'm not being a huge sucker.

"Okay, fine, but this is temporary."

She grins as she stands. "Thank you. Thank you for giving me a chance." She pumps my hand and I notice her palms are a bit sweaty. Huh. She was nervous. The mystery of Phoebe might be more intriguing than I thought.

Chapter 8

Describe your job in two words. Flabby asses. ~ Text from Hailey to Suzie

"Another day, another naked ass," I say as I hand my camera to Suzie for her to extract the pictures I took today.

She grabs the camera and switches it on to check out the pictures with a big 'ol smile on her face. I'm starting to think she's a voyeur. Her nose scrunches as she scrolls through the pictures. "Someone needs to work out more. Because that ass is the definition of flabby."

"He probably doesn't have time to work out between the two mistresses and the wife." You heard me right. He's canoodling with three women at the same time. Who has the time? Or the energy?

"Huh. You'd think that much fucking would improve the muscle tone on his ass."

Someone clears her throat behind me. "Um…"

I stand and offer a smile to Phoebe. "I didn't hear you come in."

"Do I..." She clears her throat and gestures to the camera. "I don't actually have to... you know... do I?"

My eyes widen. "No. Hell no. These are pictures from some work I did earlier today. Totally different situation."

She exhales and her shoulders drop. "Oh, good. I thought may have misunderstood. Considering the other women who were here yesterday to interview."

At the reminder of yesterday's mix-up, I glare at Suzie. She raises her hands in surrender. "Sorry, sorry. I didn't realize my ad would bring the women of the night into the daylight."

I ignore her to concentrate on Phoebe. She's dressed similarly to her outfit of yesterday. A tight dress showing off all her curves and high heels on her feet. When I stand, she towers over me. She must be at least an inch or two taller than me.

She runs her hand down her dress. "Am I dressed okay?"

Suzie snorts. "Please, your honey is going to attract all the horny bees tonight." She stands and walks from behind her desk to take a closer look at Phoebe and promptly runs into the corner of the desk and takes a nosedive to the floor. She rolls at the last moment to land on her back.

"Oh, my goodness. Are you hurt?" Phoebe bends down to help Suzie stand.

"She'll be fine. This happens all the time. You get used to it." Suzie springs to her feet. "See? All fine. Are you ready to go?"

"Are you sure I can't come with you?" Suzie begs.

"No. You can't come with." The word inconspicuous is not in Suzie's vocabulary. Which is fine, I love her for who she is. But an asset during a honey pot operation she is not.

Phoebe and I walk out of the building and climb into my SUV. "We're going to the Grand Hotel," I explain as I start the engine. It's super handy cheaters tend to flock to the same hotel. It's given me the chance to get to know most of the staff. I know who to avoid and know who's willing to do a bit of side business for an extra buck.

As we drive, I explain how we work to her. "My client... er...I guess I should say our client is Mrs. Wilson. She suspects her husband is cheating on her but has no proof. All she knows is he has drinks with his colleagues every Thursday after work at the Grand Hotel. She's not welcome to join them, and he often comes home smelling of cheap perfume."

"Oh. Should I have used cheap perfume?" Phoebe asks.

I chuckle. "You're fine." She's probably wearing some fancy-schmancy two hundred dollars an ounce stuff. I'm normally not a fan of perfume, but hers is subtle and surprisingly appealing. If I thought I could afford it, I'd ask her what it is.

I find a parking spot on the street near the hotel. "First rule. Never use the valet service. If you need to leave in a hurry, it's a disaster." Trust me. I know. Running down State Street with an angry man chasing me while screaming *I'll get you bitch* is not something I plan to ever repeat.

I park and we walk into the hotel. We must look like quite the pair. Me in my ripped jeans, t-shirt, and shitkicker boots walking with a woman dressed like a model stepping off the runway. I nod to Peggy who smiles and waves when she notices me. She also gives me two thumbs up as if she's cheering me on for some great adventure.

I direct Phoebe toward the lounge where I see Andy is working. I settle Phoebe at the bar on a barstool visible to everyone walking in. Perfect.

"This is Andy. He'll take good care of you." She looks confused. I bend forward and whisper. "He'll water down the drinks to make sure you don't end up getting drunk while you're waiting."

Another lesson learned. When I say a drunk woman does not attract a target, I am not lying. At least it wasn't me who got stinking drunk and screamed the place down about cheating men who should have their dicks chopped off. We really should screen candidates to make sure they aren't man-haters.

"What can I get you?" Andy asks as his eyes rove over her body.

I snap my fingers in his face. "No." He pouts. "No," I repeat. He will not be hitting on my employee. We're here to work.

"Vodka martini with Stolichnaya if you have it," Phoebe orders, ending my stare down with Andy.

"Coming right up." He moves away to make the drink.

"Stolichnaya?" Fancy, I think but don't say.

She shrugs. "Ever since I visited Moscow, I can't stand other vodkas."

The enigma grows. Unfortunately, I don't have time to explore the mystery of Phoebe right now. I pull a picture out of my bag. "This is our target." The man in the picture is good looking, no doubt about it. He has curly brown hair, sparkling hazel eyes, and a lopsided smile with two dimples.

"And I just sit here? You don't want me to try and attract him?"

I look her up and down. "You can maybe cross your legs when he's looking." She has fantastic legs. Nicely shaped. Unlike mine, which are pretty much two sticks that take me from A to B.

"When he approaches you, you'll need to flirt with him. Try to get him to commit to going upstairs to a room with you."

"Nothing more? I don't have to …" she leans in close and whispers, "kiss him or fondle him or anything?"

I shrug. "It helps if you kiss him when you get to the room, but there's no need for it in this case. Mrs. Wilson wants proof he's picking up women at the bar, nothing more. She specifically said she didn't want any obscene pictures."

Andy sets her drink down on the bar in front of her. "Enjoy."

Phoebe drinks half of it down in one gulp. She wrinkles up her nose. "Watered down? I don't think there's an ounce of vodka in this thing."

I pat her shoulder. "Not getting drunk, remember? It was rule number two."

"Should I be writing this down?"

I snort and walk off to get a room key from Peggy. I chat with her for a while as I wait for six o'clock, aka the witching hour when all the cheaters come out to play, to arrive. Sure enough, at five minutes past six, a group of men in suits arrive. I spot Mr. Wilson among them.

"Time to work," I tell Peg as I follow the group into the bar. I saunter past Phoebe and place the key on the bar in front of her. She nods and I keep moving. I position myself in a dark corner no one ever notices – except for couples who are too impatient to make the trip up the elevator to a room, because apparently, the entire world thinks I'm a voyeur.

From my hidey-hole, I watch as the men order drinks from the bartender. Every single one of them, wedding ring or not, glances in Phoebe's direction. I can't blame them. She is a stunner. I also don't have a problem with looking. It's the touching that crosses the line and gets you in trouble.

Mr. Wilson takes his beer from Andy and immediately zeroes in on Phoebe. This is going to be a short night. Phoebe tilts her head down and smiles from beneath her lashes at him as he approaches. Oh, she's good. I take out my camera and start taking pictures.

Fifteen minutes later, they're still flirting at the bar. *Come on, Phoebe. Seal the deal.* Wilson raises his hand to order another drink, but she grabs it as she bites her bottom lip. I can't hear what they're saying, but – judging by the excitement lighting up his eyes – she's asking him to her room. *Good girl.*

Wilson drops his hand to help Phoebe out of her chair. She grabs the keycard and looks around the bar until she spots me. I give her a thumbs-up. She nods before returning her attention to Wilson.

As soon as they are out of sight, I move. I rush to the stairwell and run up the two flights of stairs to the third floor. I open the door and listen for the elevator. It opens, and I hear Phoebe giggle. And I thought I was a good actress. I ain't got nothing on her.

Once I hear them walk down the hallway, I push through the door and follow them. They disappear behind a room door, but the door doesn't close completely. Of course, it doesn't. This isn't my first rodeo. I wait a few beats and sneak into the room behind them.

Wilson has Phoebe pressed against a wall. He's licking her neck as his hands roam up and down her sides. I snap a dozen pictures and then mouth *got it* to Phoebe. Instead of ending the charade, she looks at me with big round eyes begging me to take action. Well, damn. I forget to tell her how to get herself out of these types of situations. All she has to say is she changed her mind. If he gets violent, I have her covered. But I didn't prepare her properly. I'm an idiot.

I put my camera in my bag and take a few steps back before banging on the door. "Hello!" I saunter in as if this is my room. Wilson moves away from Phoebe to glare at me.

"What are you doing in here?" he growls.

I point to myself. "What am I doing in here?"

He stalks toward me. "Yeah, you bitch. What the fuck are you doing in here?"

I look around all befuddled. "But this is my room, I think? Isn't this room 350?" I make a huge production of looking at the number on the door. Sure enough. It's 350.

Wilson looks confused now. "I thought you said this was your room," he asks Phoebe.

She shrugs all innocent like.

I act like this is the first time I notice Phoebe in the room. "You! You're the one who bumped into me in the lobby. You took my wallet." I pretend to reach for my phone. "I'm calling the police."

Wilson holds up his hands. "This has nothing to do with me. Sorry, babe," he says to Phoebe. "Maybe another time." He rushes out of the room like his ass is on fire. Good riddance. I watch him enter the elevator before returning my attention to Phoebe whose eyes are the size of saucers.

"You did good."

Her eyes widen further. "I did?"

"Yeah, sure. We need to talk about exit strategies, though."

"Yes, please. I didn't know what to do. His slimy mouth was all over me." She shivers.

"I'm sorry. Are you okay? Are you sure this is something you can handle doing on a regular basis?" Best to ask now when the memory of his hands on her is fresh in her mind.

She waves away my concerns with a flick of her hand. "Please. Easiest job in the world."

Well, okay then. "Let's get out of here. There's a beer calling my name."

"And I'd like a drink with actual alcohol in it."

A girl of my own heart.

Chapter 9

How do you make your girlfriend scream during sex? Call and tell her about it. ~ Text from Suzie to Hailey

IT HAS BEEN A seriously long-ass day. Catching two adulterers in the act is more tiring than it sounds like. I don't bother stopping by Pops' bar tonight. Nope. I'm going straight home to a bottle of wine and a bubble bath.

I park my car in the carport and walk into the kitchen from the side entrance of the house. I don't bother flipping on a light. I head straight to the refrigerator and a bottle of wine. Something crunches under my foot. What the hell? I'm not the cleanest person in the world. But – despite what Suzie the obsessive cleaner says – I'm not a slob either. I most definitely don't leave trash on my floor.

I take a step backwards and switch on the light. "Fucking hell," I mutter when I see the mess. It looks like someone opened every single cabinet in my kitchen, flung the contents on the floor, and then stomped all over the floor to make sure every single item was broken. Talk about having a hissy fit.

I call the police and go sit in my car. I must fall asleep because the next thing I know someone's knocking on my window. I roll it down.

"You the owner?" the police officer asks and indicates my house.

"Yes." Before he can ask me to explain what happened, I tell him, "I came home and found the place trashed. I've only been in the kitchen. When I saw the mess, I called it in and came out here."

"Good job. Stay here."

He walks to the group of officers standing in my driveway and starts barking orders at them. Seconds later, they're moving. A few of the group go to the front door, while the rest go to the side door. I keep my eyes trained on my house, waiting for them to come out and tell me the place is clear. I screech and nearly jump out of my skin when someone knocks on my window again.

I place my hand on my chest to keep my heart from jumping out of my chest and swivel my head to see who knocked. Groan. Aiden, again. I can't get rid of this guy. "What are you doing here?"

He smirks. "It's nice to see you again, too."

I raise my eyebrow. "You didn't answer my question."

"Because it was a stupid question." He gestures toward the house. "Your place was broken in to?"

"Yes, I'm aware. But why are you here?" I speak slowly to make sure he understands.

His cheeks darken. "Um. I asked the desk to notify me if anything involving you or your business came up."

Now, I'm confused. "Why?"

"We still haven't figured out who broke into your office," he says as if his words explain everything.

Whatever. I'm too tired for this shit and my evening in a bath with a bottle of wine just got cancelled.

Aiden looks up and nods at the police officers streaming out of my place. "It's clear. You want to go in and see if anything was taken?"

Stupid question. Yes, I simply can't wait to go into my ransacked house and see if anything was stolen. I don't speak my sarcastic response out loud, though. Aiden may be acting friendly, but he's still a cop. I know better than to aggravate a cop. Wish he could say the same thing about me.

I simply open my car door. Aiden takes my elbow to usher me into the house. I shake him off. I don't need assistance walking into my home.

I start in the kitchen. I wouldn't be able to tell if anything is missing from here if my life depended on it. All my dishes are smashed to smithereens. I move on to the living room. The television is still in place, but my books and DVDs are scattered about the room. Every single one of my DVDs has been removed from its case. And I have a whole lot of DVDs since drama geek and movie aficionado are close cousins. But apparently, someone does not approve of my movie collection.

"I'm sorry, Hailey," Aiden says from way too close to me. I shiver at his closeness and try to cover it up by crossing my arms over my stomach as if I'm cold.

"It's fine," I say as I take a step away. I've been meaning to go digital with my collection anyway. Doesn't look like I have a choice now.

I look away from the mess and notice Aiden standing there holding his jacket out to me. "Here. You look cold."

Damn. I'm not cold. In fact, my entire body heats up when the man is near. But I wouldn't admit to my body's response if you put a gun to my head. There's no need to give him any ammunition. I take the jacket and place it over my shoulders. It smells like him, spicy with an undertone of woodsy. How does he smell like the great outdoors when we live in the city? I sniff again. I want to roll around in the scent. I look up and spot Aiden smirking at me. Busted.

I pretend not to notice his reaction and march toward the hallway and my bedroom. First, I check the hall powder room. Nothing destroyed here, although what you would destroy in a room with a toilet and sink is beyond me. I move on to my office, leaving my bedroom for last. I have a feeling whatever happened in my bedroom is going to freak me out.

I open the door to my office and nearly scream. Everything is destroyed. Completely and utterly destroyed. The drawers of my filing cabinet are open, and papers are strewn everywhere. My printer is smashed into a million pieces. The pieces of which are scattered on the floor. On the desk where my computer should be is a big fat nothing.

"My laptop is missing," I tell Aiden.

"Anything else?"

I shake my head and leave the room. I take a deep breath before opening the door to my bedroom. I look around and sigh in relief. Yes, it's a mess, but it's not a creepy mess. I was terrified I was going to walk in here and see evidence on the bedspread, if you get what I mean. But no. It's a freaking mess as if someone was searching for a specific item.

"What do you think he was looking for?"

Oops. I must have spoken my thoughts out loud. I shrug. "I have no idea."

"Come on." Aiden grabs my hand and pulls me out of the room down the hallway to the kitchen table where he pushes me into a chair. He manages to find an intact glass, fills it with water, and sets it in front of me.

I glare at the glass. "Water? Really? You think I need water right now?" I'm thinking the vodka in the freezer is what the doctor ordered.

"Finish this first," he orders.

I roll my eyes. Who is he? My dad? Oh shit, Pops. He is going to freak. Unless I don't tell him. What he doesn't know, he can't freak out about. Good plan, Hailey.

Aiden takes a seat across from me and pulls out a notebook. "Any idea what an intruder could be looking for?"

"No idea. He left all the expensive stuff. Well, except for my laptop."

"Did you keep your work on the laptop?"

"No. The laptop is for my private use."

Suzie isn't just some wacky klutz I hired. She's also a damn good business manager. She insisted I keep my work separate from my private stuff. It makes it more clear for the tax authorities or something. Not only did she make sense, but I have no desire to bring home evidence of how men can be untrustworthy. It does nothing for my faith in humanity, which is pretty non-existent anyway. Thanks, Mom.

"Do you have any enemies?" And thus, the interrogation begins. For the next however long, I answer question after question for Aiden. Most of which I answer with *I don't know.* Because I don't. I have no idea why anyone would target me.

Finally, he closes his notebook. "I think we're done for tonight. We'll delve deeper into this tomorrow."

Delve deeper? How do you delve deeper into *I don't know?*

"In the meantime, do you have somewhere you can stay tonight?"

I look at the clock. It's after midnight. I'm not calling Suzie and waking her up. "I'll check into a hotel for the night. Get this sorted out in the morning."

Suzie will be all over getting this place into tip-top shape in no time. I guess it's a good thing she convinced me to hire Phoebe to help with the filing after all.

The corners of Aiden's lips turn down. "Maybe you should stay with your dad to make sure you're safe."

I shake my head. Not happening. "There's no indication whoever this is, is after me personally." Haven't I already said this a dozen times?

"I don't like the idea of you being in danger."

"I don't like the idea much myself, but I'm not in danger." I indicate the house with a sweep of my arm. "Does this look personal to you?" I'm talking shit. Some random dude destroyed all of my belongings. It feels incredibly personal. In your face personal.

"Come on." He stands. "I'll follow your car to the hotel. Make sure you get there safe."

Whatever. I'm done arguing. "Let me put together an overnight bag."

My clothes and toiletry items might be strewn all over my bedroom and bathroom, but nothing was destroyed. I grab a sports bag from my closet and throw some stuff for an overnight stay in a hotel in it.

"Ready?" Aiden asks when I walk into the kitchen carrying a bag. He's alone. The rest of the police officers disappeared a while ago. "Let's get you to safety," he says and puts his hand in the small of my back to escort me out of my own home. And no, my body doesn't tingle all over at his touch. Really, it doesn't.

Chapter 10

What's the difference between a woman with PMS and a terrorist? You can negotiate with a terrorist. ~ Text from Pops to Hailey

As soon as I walk into McGraw's the following evening, I know I've made a mistake. The angry vibe is practically visible in the air. One look at Pops and I know why. His fury is being broadcast loud and clear from his face. Well, shit. Suzie must have tattled on me.

"Someone's got a big mouth," I grumble as I stand frozen at the entrance. I debate making a U-turn and fleeing, but I know better. I slump and shuffle my way to Pops behind the bar. As soon as I'm within arm's reach, he pulls me into his arms. He's suffocating me, but now is not the time to complain.

"Why didn't you tell me what happened, Babycakes?" he asks when he finally releases me.

I don't get a chance to contemplate my lie before my uncles join in on the action.

"Yeah, Hails, why didn't you tell us?" Lenny grumbles. Barney, Wally, and Sid nod in agreement.

"I didn't want you to worry." There are snorts all around in reaction to my words. "What? It's true."

Pops puts an arm around my shoulder and pulls me close. "We always worry about you."

"All the damn time," Lenny agrees.

"I'd be less worried if you had a man."

My eyes widen at Pops' remark. "Need I remind you, you've chased off every single man who's been interested in me since I was twelve years old."

"None of them were good enough for you." He is unrepentant.

"Yeah," Sid agrees. "You need a man who is willing to die for you. Who looks at you as if you're his whole world." Sid the romantic strikes again. I stick my finger in my mouth and pretend to gag. He frowns at me.

Lenny chuckles. "I don't know about all the gooey love stuff, but you do need a man to keep you safe."

I glare at him. How dare he say I can't protect myself! When Barney nods, I switch my glare to him. "Et tu, Brute?"

"I say we find a man for her." At Wally's suggestion, my eyes nearly bug out of my head. He can't be serious. I glare daggers at him. He holds up his hands. "What? You're thirty-one. You should have been able to find a man on your own by now."

"Need I point out how not one of you is married. Not a single one."

"Hey! I've been married," Sid argues.

"Five times. Maybe the sixth time is the charm," Barney jokes. I high-five him.

"I've only been married four times. One time was technically a common law marriage. It doesn't count," Sid explains.

"I'm pretty sure Wisconsin law says differently." You learn all kinds of stuff at those criminal justice classes.

"Anyway, we were talking about finding Hails a man, not my marriages."

"We must have some buddies who have sons who are date-able," Wally says. Is he serious about this matchmaking business?

I look to Pops and he's nodding as if he's considering it. "You can't be serious! I can take care of myself. You guys made sure of it."

I'm not kidding. They did. My self-defense skills are top-notch thanks to them. I also know how to shoot pretty much every handgun legally available and some of those not legal. Plus, I can throw a knife with a fair bit of accuracy. And, thanks to Wally, I can override most security systems. See? I've got skills.

"Still," Pops says as he puts his arms around me, "a man would take care of you in a way we can't."

I take a deep breath to control my anger. It doesn't work. "I'm a grown woman. I can take care of myself." To prove it, and because I'm more than a bit annoyed with their overprotectiveness, I grab Pops' wrist and twist it behind his back until he's pushed up against the bar with his arm at an uncomfortable angle. "See?"

Pops chuckles. "I let you."

Yeah, right. "Way to save face."

"Come on." Wally motions me. "Get a beer and tell us all about what happened."

"Buy me a hamburger and I'll think about it." Think about it? Hah. As if I have a choice in the matter.

While Pops orders me a burger and fries, the uncles usher me to 'their' booth in the corner of the bar. Yes, they have their own booth. Of course, they do. They practically live here. It's always funny when a stranger thinks he can sit here. The uncles don't say anything. They don't need to. The stares and glares they can throw anyone's way are enough to make a grown man piss himself. Seriously. I've seen it happen. And you can bet your bottom dollar I made them clean the piss up as well. I sure wasn't going to!

Pops sets a frosted mug in front of me and sits next to me. "Now, tell us everything."

I take a slug of my beer to fortify myself and then tell them everything. I'm not stupid. I know when to pick my battles.

"At least Barnes was there," Wally comments when I finish my story.

"You have got to be shitting me. You do know who Aiden Barnes is, right? The guy who tormented me throughout high school? The guy you were ready to eviscerate a few days ago? Am I ringing any bells?"

Wally shrugs. "Yeah, he's an asshole, but he looks like someone who can handle himself in a fight."

"Why didn't you come stay with me last night? Why did you go to a hotel by yourself?" Pops asks and I know he's not asking because of my safety. No, he's also hurt I didn't tell him about my problems.

"It was late."

He raises an eyebrow and looks around the bar. Rookie mistake. Of course, he's still up at midnight. McGraw's doesn't close until midnight during the week.

"I didn't want to worry you."

His eyebrow merely raises another inch. My shoulders hunch. I have no excuse. I should have at least told him what happened last night.

"Promise me you won't keep information concerning your safety from me again."

"Promise me you won't go ballistic."

He shakes his head. "I can't promise you that. You're my baby girl. Nuh-uh." He places a finger over my mouth to shut off my reply. "You'll always be my baby girl. It doesn't matter how old you are. You can be married with children and you'll still be my baby girl."

Well, damn. How can I argue with him now?

"Fine." I grunt. "I'll keep you informed."

"That's my good girl," he says before giving me a noogie.

"Hey!" I bat his hands away. "Don't ruin the hair."

The door to the bar bangs open and in walks Suzie. I stand and face her. Time to give someone a piece of my mind. The uncles hold me back.

"She was only doing what she thought was right," Pops says.

"Tattling is wrong. She could have talked to me. But no, she acted like everything was all honkey dory all day at the office and then went behind my back. Not okay."

"I say we let her go," Barney says. "I bet ten bucks Hails can take Suzie out in less than a minute."

Wally snorts. "As if anyone is going to bet against Hailey. We trained her after all."

Suzie's eyes widen when she sees the look of anger on my face. She swivels to leave and trips on her own feet.

"And down she goes!" shouts Barney.

"At least you're not clumsy like that one. How we are ever going to find a man to take care of her is beyond me," Sid says.

I snort. "Good luck. Suzie is the definition of man-hater."

"She just hasn't met the right man yet."

I don't comment. I'd love to see Sid try and set Suzie up. It would be hilarious. I may sound mean, but she's the one who tattled on me like we're fifth graders and not in our thirties.

Suzie stands and brushes herself off. I have to give her credit. She marches over to our group without a backward glance. "I'm sorry, Hails. I can't stand the thought of you being in danger."

"Why does everyone keep forgetting I'm not the target of whatever this is?"

"Yeah, right." Wally disagrees. "That's why your business *and* your house have been broken into."

"But nothing was taken and whoever it is didn't do any yucky stuff in my bedroom." I don't know who I'm trying to convince – me or them.

Pops groans and rubs a hand down his face. "Oh great, there's a visual I won't be able to erase."

"Please, forgive me," Suzie begs. "I'll clean your house for free."

She was already going to clean my house. My clean freak friend was itching to get her hands on it all day long. She probably would have demanded payment in the form of donuts and coffee, though.

"Fine." She jumps and stumbles. Once she's steady on her feet again, I point at her. "But no more. You hear me? No more going behind my back. We're a team, dammit."

"Yes!" she shouts and tackles me. She may be a little thing but she's a force of nature. I don't have a chance of keeping my feet under me. We both go down.

"Huh," Barney mutters, "good thing I didn't make those bets. Looks like little Suzie took Hailey down after all."

Chapter 11

What do you see when the Pillsbury Dough Boy bends over? Doughnuts. ~ Text from Suzie to Hailey

MY FINGERS DRUM AGAINST my desk the next morning as I wait for Aiden to show up. He wants to go over all my cases to see if there's anyone who could possibly want to target me. Total waste of time if you ask me. And I'm not excited to see the object of my teenaged fantasies again. My heart isn't beating fast and my skin is not tingling in anticipation. Really.

The door to my office bursts open and in strolls Suzie carrying a box of donuts.

"Your love of donuts is starting to border on obsession," I say as I stand to grab a cinnamon twist. Note – cinnamon twists aren't donuts and thus not subject to obsession.

"Food high in calories and fat are bad for your complexion," Phoebe adds as she walks into my office.

"It speaks!" Suzie shouts and then does a little dance.

Phoebe looks at me. "Should we call an ambulance? Is she having a fit of some kind?"

I bark out a laugh. The fashion ice queen might be fun to have around after all.

Suzie glares at Phoebe. "For that, you're joining us tonight for a girls' night out."

Phoebe stares down at Suzie who stares right back at her. My best friend may be small in stature, but she makes up for it with bucketloads of attitude. "Nuh-uh. You are not getting out of this. Glare at me all you want. I'm rubber, you're glue. Your stares bounce off of me and sticks to you."

"I don't think that's how the saying goes."

Suzie pauses her stare down with Phoebe to toss me a glare and then goes right back to her stare-down. "You are coming with us to the bar and you are having a good time. End of."

Phoebe opens her mouth to respond, but Suzie flips up her hand. "Uh oh. It's been decided."

"Knock knock," Aiden hollers as he walks into the office.

Suzie grabs the donuts and flips around to offer one to Aiden. Her feet somehow get tangled and she stumbles. Phoebe grabs hold of her upper arm to stop her from hitting the ground.

"Do I get hazard pay for working here?" Phoebe asks as she rights Suzie.

"I would have been fine on my own," Suzie lies.

Phoebe nods. "Sure."

I watch as Aiden looks Phoebe up and down. My stomach churns. Of course, he's checking her out. The woman is absolutely, positively gorgeous. She's dressed in another wrap-around dress showcasing all her assets. With high heels on her feet, she's the same height as him. Her cheeks flush as she greets him. "Detective."

"Aiden, please. Call me Aiden." He stretches out a hand to shake hers.

The churning in my stomach increases until it feels like someone threw my stomach in the spin cycle of a washing machine. I place a hand on my belly as I order it to calm the eff down. I will not act like a jealous cow. I do not want Aiden. I don't. I just have to keep reminding myself of the fact.

I swallow the lump stuck in my throat and force myself to introduce them, "Detective Barnes, this is our new employee, Phoebe Adams."

"Hi Aiden!" Suzie shouts and breaks whatever spell was being woven between Phoebe and Aiden. I don't sigh in relief when Phoebe takes a step away from him toward the door. Nope. I had a little breathing issue of some kind. It was not a sigh. Seriously.

"Donut?" Suzie sticks the box under Aiden's nose as she winks at me. *I got your back* she mouths.

Aiden takes a chocolate crème and nods his thanks to her.

Phoebe grabs Suzie's arm and pushes her out the door. "Let us know if you need anything," she says as she shuts the door.

"Hey!" I can hear Suzie's shout from the other side of the door. "It's my job to take care of her needs."

I feel my face heat at the innuendo of Suzie's words. "Anyway." I clear my throat. "How can I help you today?" As if I don't know perfectly well why he's here.

Aiden takes a seat at the chair across from my desk. "I think we should go through your cases. See if there's anyone who has a reason to target you."

This again. "No one is targeting me." He starts to argue with me, but I hold up my hand to stop him. "Seriously. Think about it. My office was ransacked at night when no one was here. My house was ransacked when I wasn't home as well."

"But you could have been home. In fact, based on the time of the break-in at your house, you should have been home."

Little does he know. I'm almost never home in the evening. I'm either out hunting skirt chasers or I'm at Pops' bar. "Nothing about this spells personal. I think whoever is doing this is looking for something." It can't be personal. It just can't.

"What do you think they're looking for?" Aiden opens his notebook and pulls out a pen as if I'm going to give him a list. Hardly.

"I have no idea."

He tilts his head and raises his eyebrow. "Seriously? You have no idea?" He snorts as if he doesn't believe me. "You don't think there's a possibility some man you caught cheating is after the proof of his infidelity. Some man who is being taken to the cleaners in his divorce due to pictures you took."

Not this again. "But we don't keep proof of any man's infidelity here."

He looks confused "But that's what you do, isn't it? You take pictures of cheaters. You Cheat, We Eat?"

I roll my eyes. "Yes, of course. But we don't keep the pictures."

"Explain."

"Okay, here's how it works. I take the pictures. Suzie prints them and sends them to the client. We don't keep copies of the pictures in our files. We only keep the background research, my notes, which prove absolutely nothing, and the client invoices."

"Here's the thing." Aiden leans forward. "No one knows about this procedure except for you and Suzie."

Damn. He's right. Well, shit.

Aiden smirks as if he's confident in my impending capitulation. "Let's go through your files and see who has motive to find those pictures."

I haven't capitulated yet, though. "Why are you making a big deal of this? I know how the police work. This case has to be a low priority and yet, here you are, spending precious time talking to me, going over cases."

"You don't get it, do you?"

I huff. Obviously not.

"I don't want you to be in danger."

"I'm not in danger!" I'm starting to sound like a broken record.

He growls as he leans forward. "You don't know that for sure. Just because you got lucky twice doesn't mean you're not in danger. Obviously, he didn't find what he's looking for, and I doubt he's going to give up."

"Fine! We'll go through my case files." I stand and stomp to the door. I open it, and Suzie falls into the room. Someone is a crappy eavesdropper. "Did you not hear me stomping toward the door?"

"I thought maybe you were stomping toward Aiden. Angry sex is the hottest sex."

"Angry sex!" I squeak. "Why would I be having sex with Aiden in my office in the morning?"

Suzie rolls her eyes. "Because he's hot and you've had a crush on him since tenth grade."

I'm going to slap her. Seriously. Slap the living shit out of her. No woman on a jury will convict me for battery. Not when Suzie broke the girl code in such a spectacular fashion.

Phoebe arrives and pulls Suzie until she's out of the danger zone. I continue to glare daggers at her. When the daggers don't work, I engage my lasers. They seem to be malfunctioning as well. I take a step forward, but Phoebe stands in my way.

"It's not worth it. There's a cop right behind you."

Whoops. I forgot all about Aiden. My face heats, and I'm sure I'm as red as a lobster when I turn around and offer him the fakest smile possible. "I'm going to go get those files for you," I announce before escaping.

I spend fifteen minutes in the file room pulling the files of our clients for the previous three months. Actually, I spend five minutes pulling files and then ten minutes staring out of the window debating whether I can climb out of it before Aiden realizes I'm gone.

"You're going to have to go in there sometime," Phoebe says from right behind me.

I jump. "Shit. You scared me."

She shoves the files at me until I'm forced to take them in my arms or let everything scatter to the floor. "Go in there and get it over with."

"But—"

She shakes her head. "No excuses."

"But he knows about *you know*."

She giggles. "Are you trying to tell me that man in there doesn't know you had a crush on him in high school?"

"Well…" Of course, he did. The entire freaking school did. Thus, the stupid nickname Heartsick Hailey.

"You are an adult woman. Straighten your back and march yourself into your office like you own the freaking world." When I don't start moving, she raises an eyebrow and crosses her arms over her chest. "Unless you're too chicken."

"Fine." I don't march back into my office. I stomp because apparently whenever Aiden is around, I revert back to an idiot teenager.

"Let's do this," I practically yell at him before dumping the files on my desk.

Chapter 12

Why did the ketchup blush? Because he saw the salad dressing. ~ Text from Hailey to Pops

"Do you think she'll show?" Suzie asks with her eyes trained on the front door of McGraw's Pub.

"It's not like you gave her a choice."

Suzie spent the day prancing around like a chicken whenever Phoebe gave the slightest indication she wasn't planning on coming to girls' night out with us. Frankly, I can't blame her for being apprehensive. Suzie can be a bit much to take at times.

"Hey, Suze," Pops greets as he walks toward us.

He doesn't bother asking her what she wants to drink. Why would he? Suzie spends nearly as much time here as I do. He pours her a Guinness and sets it in front of her. She sips it and swirls the liquid in her mouth as if she's taste testing it. As if she hasn't drunk a gazillion gallons of the Irish stout by now.

"Suzie!" Sid shouts as he enters the bar and walks our way. "When are you going to make an honest man of me?" He places his hand over his heart and bats his eyelashes.

Suzie giggles. "You couldn't handle me if you tried."

Wally grunts. "And the insurance premiums would kill him."

"Hey!" She takes a swipe at him but almost falls off her bar stool. He grabs her shoulders to right her while shaking his head.

"How is sex like air?" Barney asks as he joins our group.

"They're both free," Suzie guesses.

Sid grunts. "Sex is never free."

Barney looks around but no one ventures another guess. "Neither one is a big deal unless you aren't getting any." He laughs at his own joke and I reach over to high-five him.

"What are you two doing here tonight?" Lenny asks. "You haven't had any more trouble, have you?"

I roll my eyes. "No."

"Has the detective made any discoveries?" Wally asks.

"Yeah, Hails. Has the detective discovered anything?" Suzie mimics. "You spent enough time with him behind closed doors today."

I glare at her. As if she hasn't caused enough problems by reminding Aiden of my crush. I was a bumbling mess as we went through the files. For once, Aiden didn't use my embarrassment against me. He pretended like everything was perfectly normal. And him being sweet didn't make my heart go pitter-patter. Nope.

"I thought you were out of the country," I address Wally and ignore Ms. Big Mouth. Wally often travels to unknown places for his work.

"Nope. I'm not taking any assignments until your situation is settled."

"You can't do that. I don't want my little problem to affect your work."

Wally grunts. "It's done. No reason to talk about it further."

He hates talking about his work, which only serves to make me curious as all get out. The man is a vault, though. He doesn't give a single thing away. I only know he travels out of the country because he brought me a birthday present from Paris once. He claimed to have bought it in New York City, but I know how to Google. I know that particular Louis Vuitton bag is not sold in stores in the U.S.

"Um." Phoebe clears her throat. "Suzie? Hailey?"

As one, the group of men turn to study Phoebe, whose eyes widen as she takes them in. Her hands tremble as she clasps them together before taking a cautious step back.

"You're here!" Suzie jumps off her chair, lurches forward, and pulls Phoebe into a hug. "You came!"

I sigh as I stand. Poor Phoebe looks like she's about to pass out. I pull Suzie away from her. "Let the woman breathe." I take her hand. "This is my family." I point to each of my uncles in turn. "Lenny. Barney. Wally. Sid." Their eyes narrow as they study her. Oh boy, here we go.

"Last name," Wally demands.

"Nope." A last name will make it easier for him to conduct a background search. I motion to Pops. "And this handsome devil is my Pops."

Pops smiles at her. "What can I get you, Phoebe?"

"Um…" Her eyes scan the bar. "A beer?"

I roll my eyes. "Make her a vodka martini with Stolichnaya."

"I don't want to put him out," she whispers.

"Please. A martini is not a big deal. We even have the proper cocktail glasses."

"But…" She trails off. I squeeze her hand to encourage her. After a moment, she nods to Pops.

Suzie motions to Pops. "Have you seen her pops? He's a total DILF. Women flock to the bar. He can prepare any frou-frou drink you can think of."

Pops cheeks flame, but he chuckles as he sets the martini on the bar top. "Why don't you ladies grab a booth and I'll put an order in for some nachos?"

"And maybe some veg and hummus."

Pops screeches to a halt, and the uncles swivel their heads to stare at me. "Not for me," I explain. "Phoebe is a health nut."

"I wouldn't say health nut," she denies.

I raise an eyebrow. "Then you do want nachos?"

She clears her throat. "A platter of vegetables with hummus would be lovely."

We choose a booth on the opposite side of the bar from my uncles' table. I wouldn't put it past them to spend the entire evening eavesdropping on us.

We barely have a chance to sit before Suzie begins interrogating Phoebe. "Are you from Milwaukee? You don't sound like a native Wisconsinite. You have some accent I can't place. Where is your accent from? Are you single? Do you have any children? How old are you?"

Subtle is not a word you can apply to Suzie. "Give her a chance to breathe, will you?" The poor woman is still shaking from meeting the uncles.

The door opens, and I watch as Aiden strolls in the bar. He takes one step inside and is immediately surrounded by the uncles. Damn. Now, I have to save him.

"Officer Barnes," I shout as I walk to the group. "Did you want to see me?"

"Yeah, Barnes." Wally mimics me. "Did you want to see Hailey?"

I elbow him. "He's the officer assigned to my case, remember? He's not a suitor."

Sid growls. "Why not? Does he think he's too good for you?"

My uncles do my head in. "Come on." I lead Aiden to an empty table in the middle of the bar where I can keep my eye on my uncles and Pops at the same time. Pops hasn't said a thing, but he's staring at Aiden as if he stole the last bottle of Guinness in the place.

"Did you discover any leads in my case?" I ask once we're seated.

"Well, hello, Hailey. It's nice to see you, too. I'm doing fine. Thanks for asking."

I roll my eyes. "Sarcasm does not look good on you, Barnes." I'm lying. The man looks good in anything. Hell, he could scream the alphabet while drunk wearing a diaper and he'd still look hot. Nope. Shake those thoughts of a near-naked Aiden right out of your head, Hailey. I've had just the one beer. Honest.

"I've checked out about half of the clients, but I've got bupkis thus far." I open my mouth to say *I told you so*, but he doesn't give me a chance. "I still have thirty clients to check out."

I stand. "Well, thanks for coming by to update me personally. Grab a beer on me before you leave."

Aiden grabs my wrist before I can make my escape. My skin tingles and heat flows from my wrist straight to my lady bits. I pull my hand away before he can notice the effect he has on me. Judging by the smirk on his face, I wasn't quick enough.

"Sit down. I'm not done."

I drop into the chair like a petulant teenager. "Do you have another lead?"

"I don't want to talk about the case."

In that case. I try to stand again but he growls at me, and my body – my stupid body – refuses to move. This is not a good sign. "What do you want to talk about then?"

"Me taking you out. Us."

"There is no us."

"Only because you won't give me a chance."

I lean forward and hiss at him. "I don't need your pity."

His eyes widen. "Who said anything about pity?"

"Why else would you be here asking me out?" And then before I can tell my mouth to shut the hell up, I continue. "You couldn't run away from me fast enough in high school. What's changed?"

"I told you. You don't know the entire story about high school. I didn't bully you. I protected you. I can prove it to you. Let me prove it to you." He reaches forward and places his hand over mine. His thumb caresses my wrist and goosebumps explode across my skin.

"Give him a chance," Sid shouts from the other side of the bar.

"How do you even know what he asked?"

Wally holds up a bionic ear listening device.

"Pops doesn't like him." I smirk. Best excuse ever.

"I only said I didn't like him to push you together," Pops explains to the entire bar because of course, the entire bar has quieted down in order for all the patrons to follow every single word being said. Oh good. I'm glad this isn't embarrassing.

"Fat lot of good that did."

Pops chuckles. "You are the most stubborn daughter in the universe."

"Say yes," Suzie shouts. The entire bar picks up the chant. *Say yes! Say yes!*

"Fine!" I yell and stand. "I will go out with you one time. But if you can't prove you didn't bully me in high school, I will sic my uncles on you." I lift my chin at my uncles, and they nod in agreement.

"No one bullies our Hailey," Lenny announces as he glares at Aiden.

"Oh good." Aiden stands. "No pressure for our first date then."

"First and only," I shout at him.

"You can keep telling yourself that, Hails. But I know the truth."

"One date!" I scream, but he's already gone.

I stomp my foot and walk back to the booth where Suzie is clapping, and Phoebe looks like she's ready to bolt. She's on her own. I have a date with Jose. He's a very good friend of mine. No salt or lime necessary.

Chapter 13

"What did the elephant say to the naked man? How do you breathe through that thing?" ~ Text from Hailey to Suzie

"Did you notice how Phoebe didn't answer any questions about herself last night?"

At Suzie's question, I groan. Why is she talking? My head feels like it's going to explode. I love Jose, but he can be a bit of an asshole on the day after we hook up. "Can you talk softer?"

"Did you notice how Phoebe didn't answer any questions about herself last night?" she whispers.

I lay my head on my desk and use my hands to cover it. I don't answer Suzie's question. I can't. I don't remember much about last night after the first three shots of tequila.

"Anyway, I did a background check on her."

What? I expect my uncles and Pops to pull this kind of stunt. Not Suzie. I manage to open one eye and glare at her. "Are you serious?"

"You can't be mad. We should do background checks on all our employees. It's normal practice."

Damn. She's right. Fine. "What did you find out?" I manage to croak out my question. Did someone stuff a bunch of cotton balls down my throat last night?

"Phoebe Adams didn't exist until a year ago."

"Hold up." I force myself to sit up. I have to grab hold of the edge of the desk to keep steady. My stomach revolts and I take deep breaths to settle it. When I'm sure I don't need to make a run to the porcelain god, I ask, "What are you saying?" She hands me a bottle of water. I down about half of it before asking, "What do you mean she didn't exist until a year ago?"

"Exactly what I said. Phoebe Adams did not exist last year. No driver's license, no utility bills. Nothing. Nada. Rien."

"Well, shit." I chug the rest of my water as I try to formulate a response. "What should we do?"

Suzie looks around to make sure we're alone, as if someone is going to magically appear in the office, before coming closer to whisper, "Do you think she's in witness protection?"

I shrug. "If she is, we shouldn't stick our noses into her background and raise red flags."

"I'll ask Wally to check."

"No, you won't. If she's in WITSEC and he goes digging around, whoever she testified against might find her."

Suzie pouts. "But how else are we going to find out who she testified against?"

"You don't even know if she testified against anyone. You're making assumptions. For all we know, she's a criminal on the run herself."

Her eyes widen. "Then, we definitely need Wally to snoop. We can't have a criminal working for us."

I'm an idiot. Why did I bring up the possibility of Phoebe being a criminal? Stupid. I decide to change the subject. "Why are we here anyway?" It's Saturday before noon. I should be suffering in my bed in private like any respectable hungover woman. "We usually aren't open on Saturdays." I've been known to do some sneaking around after cheaters on the weekends but come into the office? No, thank you.

"This potential client couldn't meet at any other time."

Whatever. I lay my head back on the desk. "Let me know when he arrives."

"She," Suzie informs me. The alarm beeps. "And I think she's here."

Yippee.

Suzie hands me a breath mint and another bottle of water. "Toughen up, buttercup. You're the one who decided to empty the bar of tequila last night."

Please. Not possible. Pops keeps a steady supply of hard liquor in his stockroom.

She bounces out of the room to greet our prospective client. "Hi! I'm Suzie Langley. Come on through. The private investigator is waiting to meet you." Waiting to die is more like it.

I pop the breath mint in my mouth and force myself to stand. My legs feel like I'm a newborn foal standing for the very first time, but I manage to get to my feet and stay upright. I smile as a middle-aged woman walks in. She's wearing a button-down blue and white striped shirt buttoned all the way to her neck and tucked into her baggy jeans. Her hair is poofy and held back from her face with a wide white hairband. Oh great, another woman done wrong.

Suzie gives me a thumbs-up before closing the door. I'm surprised she's leaving me alone with the client. The nosy woman hates leaving me alone with clients. The only reason I manage to get any privacy in my office at all is her duty to answer the phone.

"Hi. I'm Hailey McGraw." I shake her hand.

"Debbie Monroe," she introduces herself.

"Please, have a seat." I motion to the chair in front of my desk. Once we're both seated, I get started. "How can I help you today?"

"I need you to find out what my cat is up to when I'm at work." Not a cheating husband after all then.

My brow wrinkles. "Did you say cat?" Please, please, please, let me have heard her wrong.

"Yes." She nods and places her hands primly in her lap. Oh boy. The middle-aged woman has taken a trip to Crazyville.

"Can I ask you why you need to have your cat followed?"

"I think Fifi has a boyfriend." I hope Fifi is the name of the cat.

"And you don't want Fifi to have a boyfriend?"

She tuts. "Of course, I want Fifi to have a boyfriend. A boyfriend I approve of."

I cough to hide the laugh dying to burst from me. Crazy cat lady needs to approve her cat's boyfriend. Just when you think you've heard it all.

"I take it you let your cat roam outside while you are at work." I wait for her nod before continuing. "If you're concerned Fifi is getting into boy trouble, why don't you keep her inside?"

"I can't do that! Poor Fifi would be bored to tears if she couldn't roam around the neighborhood during the day."

Poor Fifi needs to get away from crazy cat lady is what needs to happen. "If you're worried Fifi is going to have kittens, you could always have her fixed."

"Have her fixed?" Debbie clutches her non-existent pearls. "Fixed? Like she's some poor animal." I'm confused. Are we not talking about her cat? Is cat a euphemism for something else? "Besides, I want Fifi to have kittens someday, just not with the boy she's currently running around with."

"Perhaps you could approach the cat's owner and explain."

Debbie grins. "Finally! You understand. This is why I need you. I need you to follow Fifi. Find out who this tomcat is she's involved with and stop this nonsense."

I hear Suzie start sneezing like a maniac. "Achoo! Achoo! Achoo!" Those are the worst fake sneezes I've ever heard.

I stand to go see what the hell her problem is when my phone buzzes. I look down to see a message. *Tell her you're allergic to cats!* Have I mentioned Suzie is brilliant?

I frown at Debbie. "I'm sorry to hear about Fifi's problems, but I'm afraid I can't help you. I'm allergic to cats."

"But surely you can follow Fifi without getting too close."

"But how would I ever catch the scoundrel cat who has been taking advantage of Fifi? I would need to get close to him to see his collar, so I could get in touch with his owners." I shake my head as if I'm disappointed I can't help her. See what I mean about acting coming in handy in my job?

"Oh. This is disappointing. You came highly recommended."

I stand and walk to the door of my office. Hint. Hint. Crazy cat lady, it's time to go. Debbie stands and follows me. "Good luck with Fifi. I'm sure it will all work out in the end."

I shut the door on Debbie and then turn my glare on Suzie. "You couldn't have talked to Ms. Cat Lady before making an appointment," I hiss. "I came here on a Saturday for this."

Suzie giggles. "She wouldn't tell me what the issue was on the phone. She said it was a delicate matter." She jumps out of her seat and bounces toward me. Her seat goes flying behind her and runs into the wall before bouncing back and crashing into her legs. She carries on like nothing happened. "Now, onto more important matters."

I shut off the lights and usher her out of the office while shaking my head. "Nope. I'm done for the day. I'm going home and climbing into my bed, a bed I should have never left."

"Oh, okay. I'll come over tonight then."

I stop and swivel around to look at her. "Come over tonight? Why would you come over tonight?" Not like Suzie isn't welcome at my house, but me and my hangover need some alone time.

She snorts. "To help you dress for your date with Aiden, of course."

Crap. I forgot all about my date with Aiden. After he and the entire bar forced me to say yes, I assumed I would get a reprieve. Wrong. He texted me not an hour later to let me know he'd pick me up at seven tonight.

"I can dress myself. I am an adult, you know."

Suzie puts her arm through my elbow, and we skip down the hall to the elevator. Correction. She skips. I walk like a normal person.

"Now, now. I'll help you with your make-up and hair and everything."

She sounds innocent. She's not. I know what she wants. She wants to be there when Aiden shows up. Then, she can watch me squirm and most likely embarrass myself. Not if I can help it.

"Sorry, Suzie. I'm benching you on this one."

She sticks her bottom lip out and pouts. "But I'm going to miss all the fun."

"Tell you what. As soon as you agree to date someone, I'll let you come over and help me dress for a date."

My words shut her right up. The woman does not date. Men are evil in her opinion. They're good for one thing and one thing only. Which begs the question why she's pushing me toward Aiden. Because she's a hypocrite is why. Love is okay for everyone but her. Somehow in her head, it makes sense. I've stopped trying to figure her out.

"At least take a selfie when you're ready."

Whatever. I have more important things to worry about than whether Suzie approves of my date outfit. Like the date itself. I do not want to date Aiden Barnes. My stomach tingles. Nope. I glare at it. You will not get butterflies because your high school crush asked you out. You hear me, stomach!

Chapter 14

How are buying a new car and online dating the same? With either one, you want the youngest model with the least amount of miles on it. ~ Text from Hailey to Suzie

I STARE AT MYSELF in the mirror and give myself a lecture. *Hailey McGraw, you need to stop acting like a lovesick fool whenever Aiden is near.* It's starting to get embarrassing. I snort. Starting to? This shit was embarrassing fifteen years ago in high school. Get a grip, Hailey. My lecture gets cut off when the doorbell rings. He's early. Of course, he's early.

Deep breaths, Hailey. You got this. You can go out on a date with Aiden Barnes and not make a fool of yourself. I paste on a smile and open the door. My smile freezes on my face when I get a look at him. Holy hot guy!

His red button-down shirt shows off his tanned skin, the shirt stretching across his chest as if it's barely able to keep his muscles contained. I bet he has six-pack abs. And wouldn't I love to lick each and every one. My eyes travel further and notice his thighs straining against his jeans. My hands itch to touch. Bad hands.

I look up and notice Aiden smirking. I roll my eyes. Whatever.

"Hi, Aiden."

He bends forward and kisses my cheek. "Hailey. You look lovely." Lovely is pushing it, but I do scrub up nicely. I put on a dress and everything. I even got a thumbs up from Suzie when I sent her a selfie of my outfit.

A bouquet of roses is suddenly forced upon me. "These are for you."

Guess I was too busy checking out the man to notice the flowers. Oops. "Thanks. I'll put these in the kitchen and then I'm ready. Be right back." I grab the bouquet and walk to the kitchen. Once there, I throw the flowers into the sink. Then, I cover my face with my hands and jump up and down. *Oh my god! Oh my god! I'm going out with Aiden Barnes!*

"You okay in there?" Aiden shouts from the front door.

Shit. Shit. Shit. Did he hear me? Deep breath. I'm a normal woman going out on a normal date with a normal guy. Everything is perfectly normal. Normal. "Everything's fine," I say as I walk back to him.

He grabs my hand and leads me to his SUV. He opens the door and I climb in. Huge advantage of being tall. I can get into these monster vehicles without needing assistance.

Once we're on the road, I ask, "Where are we going?"

"Have you tried the new family-style restaurant in Brewers' Hill?" I shake my head. "I thought you might like it as it's all you can eat, but they serve your table. It's not a buffet."

I gasp. "Are you saying I'm a pig?"

His eyes widen. "Um, no. But I know you like to eat."

"Then, you are saying I'm a pig?"

He's reaching panic mode now. "No, no, no. We'll go somewhere else. It was a stupid idea."

I can't hold it in anymore. I burst out laughing. "Oh my god. You should have seen your face."

He shakes his head, but there's a grin on his face. "I love your laugh. You should laugh more often."

I laugh all the time. Just not when he's around because I turn into a tongue-tied idiot in his presence.

When we arrive at the restaurant, the parking lot is packed, but Aiden manages to find a parking spot near the door. I grab the door handle to jump out, but he stops me. "Wait." I remove my hand from the handle. If he wants to play the gentleman, who am I to stop him?

Aiden opens the door and puts his big hands on my waist. He pulls me forward out of my seat and lowers me to the ground, making sure my body slides down his the entire way. My body lights up like it's the Fourth of July. I feel warm and I'm sure my face is bright red.

He smirks before making sure I'm steady on my feet. He doesn't release me, though. Instead, he leans forward and brushes his lips against mine. My eyes fall closed and my body sways closer to his. He kisses my forehead. "Come on, Hails. Let me feed you."

My stomach growls in agreement and he chuckles. Before I have a chance to die of embarrassment, he grabs my hand and pulls me in the direction of the restaurant. The place has somewhat of a bar vibe with its brick walls and brewery memorabilia on the walls, although the tables are decorated with checkered tablecloths and chianti bottle candleholders adding a romantic touch.

The hostess leads us to a booth in the corner. We don't speak as we get settled and look over the menus. The waitress arrives and we order beers to drink and something to eat.

"She must think a football team is joining us." I may have gone overboard with ordering.

"Who cares what she thinks?"

I nearly roll my eyes. Of course, Aiden Barnes doesn't care what anyone else thinks. Me on the other hand? I care entirely too much what people think, especially this man sitting across from me.

"Tell me about your job."

"What's there to tell? I catch men cheating on their wives. End of story."

"Surely, you catch women cheating as well?"

I shrug. "Sometimes. But it's mostly the gender with dicks who act like dicks and cheat."

He chuckles. "You must have seen some strange cases."

"You have no idea," I start and then proceed to tell them about Mr. and Mrs. 'Smith'.

When I finish, he stares at me with his mouth hanging open. "Let me get this straight. They pay you five-hundred bucks to catch them cheating?" He snorts. "And here I thought your job was boring."

Boring? No, my job is many things, but boring is not one of them. "It's not funny. It makes me feel like a voyeur."

He chuckles but then realizes I'm not joking. His face is dead serious as he leans forward and grasps my hand in his. "Hailey, honey, do you enjoy watching?"

I make a face and stick my tongue out. "No."

"Then, you're not a voyeur."

"But—"

He places a finger over my lips. "No. A voyeur is someone who enjoys watching other people have sex. You don't. You have nothing to feel guilty for."

He hit the nail on the head. While Suzie thinks Smith day is freaking hilarious, I can't enjoy the little game they play as I feel guilty for getting paid to set the entire thing up. "Thank you."

"You're welcome."

The waitress arrives with our food. She sets plate after plate on the table. A large salad, a basket of garlic bread, a bowl of spaghetti, a plate of bruschetta, and a pizza. My eyes widen as the table fills. I wait until she leaves before remarking, "I think we may have ordered too much."

Aiden chuckles as he scoops salad onto my plate. I allow him to eat for a few minutes before I decide it's time.

"You promised to prove you didn't bully me in high school."

"You want to do this now?"

"Yes," I say even though I don't want to do this ever. I'm thirty-one-years old I should be over how I was bullied in high school, but I'm not. At least not when it concerns this gorgeous specimen of a man sitting across from me.

"Okay." He sets down his fork and focuses on me. I squirm. "I know my clique teased you because you had a crush on me."

"Teased? Is that what we're calling it now?" Teasing is making jokes amongst people who like and respect each other. Harassing a girl to the point she runs away bawling her eyes out is not teasing.

Aiden's cheeks turn pink. "Sorry, you're right. It wasn't teasing. It was intended to be cruel." He waits for my nod before continuing. "I didn't want them to give you a hard time. I tried to stop them, but it was impossible when you followed me around like you did."

My face flames. It's true. I followed Aiden around like a lovesick puppy.

"Instead, I avoided you. If you and I weren't in the same place, they couldn't bully you about your crush on me."

My eyes widen. Is he an idiot? "Do you seriously believe they left me alone when you weren't around?"

"I know they didn't. But I figured they wouldn't be as hard on you when I wasn't around."

Whatever he thought – wrong or not – doesn't matter. What does matter is his promise to prove his innocence to me. Something all this talk is not doing. "How is this proving you didn't bully me? You may not have said the cruel words they did, but you didn't stop them either."

"I know. I apologize. I was a stupid teenager. I thought being cool was the most important thing in the world." He snorts. "I know better now."

I set my fork down and lean back in my seat. He hasn't said anything I didn't know. He already told me how he avoided me to keep his so-called friends from harassing me. Can I really blame him for not sticking up for me? He didn't know me from Adam in high school. And being cool *was* the most important thing in the world then. Ugh. I rub a hand down my face. I need to get over this obsession I have with how I was treated in high school.

"There's more." I lift my head, and my eyes practically bug out of my head when he dangles a chain in front of me.

"Is that—?" I shake my head. It can't be.

"Yeah, I attached the dog tag you had made to my actual dog tags. I wore it the entire time I was in the Army."

"You did?"

When I was a lovesick high schooler and found out Aiden was planning to join the military after graduation, I had a dog tag engraved with a quote from Vince Lombardi, considered the greatest football coach of all-time by all Wisconsinites – *Before I can embrace freedom, I should be aware of what duties I have.* I broke into Aiden's locker – having ex-military uncles is extremely useful – and put the dog tag in there. I always wondered why I didn't get harassed about my gift.

Damn. How can I not forgive him when he took my gift and kept it close to him all those years? Did he think of me when he looked at it? I put the kibosh on those thoughts. It doesn't matter. We're moving on. Starting now.

"Okay. I forgive you. I promise I'll try not to bring up our high school years any longer." Notice I said I'll try. I'm a woman. It's my prerogative to bring up shit decades old when we fight.

"Thank you." He leans across the table to kiss my forehead.

We finish our meal – which is delicious by the way – and he drives me home. I'm not inviting him in. I'm not. My body might be ready to jump him, but my head and heart need more time. He walks me to my front door.

"Thank you for a lovely evening."

He smirks before grabbing my hips and pulling me close. "You're welcome," he whispers as his head slowly descends. My eyes stare at his mouth as I lick my lips in anticipation. He groans before smashing his lips to mine. I gasp and he takes the opportunity to thrust his tongue into my mouth. I drop my purse and reach up to grab his shoulders to pull him closer.

He tilts his head as his tongue explores deeper into my mouth. I moan. He tastes even better than I imagined he could all those years ago.

"Shit." He pulls away.

I'm disorientated and puffing for breath. "What? Why are you stopping?"

"Phone," he grunts before grabbing the offending object. "What?" He listens for a few seconds before his face falls. "One sec." He places the phone against his chest. "I'm sorry, honey, I need to get to work."

"Okay." I sigh. "Be safe."

He kisses my forehead. "Thank you." Before I have a chance to ask him what he's thanking me for, he waves and jogs down the sidewalk to his SUV while talking into his phone.

Chapter 15

Why was the electrician excited to go shopping with his wife? She said they were going to the outlet mall. ~ Text from Hailey to Suzie

I'M OFF TO SHOP for new dishware and glasses on Sunday. I may be a woman, but the mall is not my favorite place to be, especially not on a Sunday when every single teenager in the city is hanging out here. I grit my teeth and force myself out of my car. I can't not go shopping. I have exactly one intact glass and zero dishes. I've been using paper plates and mugs all week. The environment will not thank me.

Suzie volunteered to join me, but I am not an idiot. I know better than to shop with my best friend. The woman thinks shopping is a game and you win when you have the most items in your cart. I'd probably end up going home with an entire new kitchen by the time she left the homeware store. No, thanks. My phone pings as I enter the store.

Had a great time last night. Sorry had to leave.
No worries. Had a great time 2.

I put my phone away, assuming our chat is finished. In my experience, men aren't big on texting. Pops would rather clean the toilets at the bar than text. Slight exaggeration but you get my point. My phone pings again.

When can I see you again?

I squeal when I read the text. *Play it cool, Hailey. Play it cool.*
emoji of woman shrugging her shoulders
Shit. Work calls. Later, honey.

I'm not ashamed to admit my lady bits sigh when he calls me honey. I force myself to put my phone back into my purse and get back to the task at hand. Replacing stuff some idiot burglar destroyed. What was he looking for anyway? And will I ever know?

I'm dragging when I walk into the office on Monday morning. I spent entirely too much time chatting with Aiden last night. I feel giddy like a teenager with her first crush. What am I saying? Aiden was my first crush. But this isn't a crush. No, this is something more. I think. Maybe?

"Good morning, Lover Girl!" Suzie greets when I open the door. I may have been able to convince her to not come over on Saturday night before my date with Aiden, but she showed up Sunday afternoon and wouldn't leave until I gave her every last detail.

"Coffee," I mumble.

"You need to buy a coffee maker."

I jump and spin around at Phoebe. "Shit. I didn't hear you come up behind me. What are you? A ninja?"

"Yeah, Phoebe, are you a ninja?" Suzie asks with a gleam in her eye that spells disaster.

Before she can start throwing questions at Phoebe, I stop her with a question of my own. "What time is the prospective client arriving?"

Suzie looks at her watch. "She should be here in fifteen minutes."

"This better not be another cat lady." I glare at her. We get some strange requests here – case in point the 'Smiths' – but a woman asking me to tail her cat was a new one. And not one I'm anxious to have repeated.

"Ms. Bostwick sounded lovely."

Yeah, right. "I'm sure Debbie Monroe sounded lovely on the telephone as well."

I grab a coffee from Suzie's desk and walk to my office to catch up on paperwork before the prospective client arrives.

I'm staring at my computer and wondering if I can get away with killing Suzie for making me review this spreadsheet when there's a knock on my office.

"You're ten o'clock is here," Suzie announces before opening the door.

I stand to greet the potential client and nearly stumble when I get a look at her. The woman is dressed like she's ready to board her private jet. I thought Phoebe was over the top with her clothes, but Phoebe has nothing on this woman. Even I know the Hermes tote she's carrying is worth over $4,000. She reaches out to shake my hand and my eyes widen when I notice the diamond-encrusted Tag Heuer watch, which must be worth at least $5,000.

What the hell is this woman doing here? In my office? Our clients aren't normally destitute, but we definitely don't cater to the rich and famous.

"Ms. Bostwick, please have a seat." I motion to a chair before taking my place behind my desk. "How can I help you today?"

"I need you to prove I'm not a murderer." My mouth drops open. Never in a million years would I have expected those words to come out of this woman's mouth.

"Not a murderer?"

She clears her throat. "I'm sure you've heard about the murder of my husband, Phillip Bostwick."

Aha. No wonder her last name sounded familiar. The murder of Phillip Bostwick is major news. The man was a billionaire business owner, although I'm not sure what businesses he owned. It's all way above my paygrade.

"I didn't know you'd been accused of his murder."

"I haven't been. Not yet anyway. It's only a matter of time."

My phone pings and I look down to see a message from Suzie. *Ask if she did it! Inquiring minds want to know.*

I'm not going to ask this woman if she killed her husband. How rude!

"And you want me to prove you didn't murder him?"

"Yes." She bobs her head. "Exactly."

"I think you may be a bit confused as to what we do here at *You Cheat, We Eat.*"

"I can pay you. I have my own money."

I hold up my hand to stop her. "Money is not the issue. I'm not qualified to investigate a murder."

"Are you sure? You come highly recommended. And I would prefer to have a woman investigate my case."

"I'm sorry." I stand. "I can't help you."

"Well." She stands as well. "Thank you for your time."

"Good luck. And my condolences on the loss of your husband."

She nods and leaves the office without saying another word. As soon as the outer door closes on the poor woman, Suzie and Phoebe invade my office.

"You should totally take her case," Suzie says.

"Are you out of your mind? I have no idea how to solve a murder case."

"Pish posh. I'm sure Aiden can help you. Think of all the money."

Phoebe sighs. "At least she was smart enough to keep her own money separate from her husband's."

She sounds like she's speaking from experience. Unfortunately, Suzie catches on to that little tidbit as well.

"Are you married, Phoebe? Or involved with someone? Is he rich? Is that how you can afford your fancy-schmancy clothes?"

"Suzie, enough! Leave the woman alone. If she wants you to know about her past, she'll tell you."

Suzie pouts. "But I want to know now."

I direct my gaze on Phoebe. "I'm sorry. I swear she doesn't mean to be a brat."

Phoebe's smile is shaky but at least she doesn't run away. "I need to get back to the filing," she says and rushes out of the room without a backward glance. So much for not running away.

Suzie collapses in a chair. "Well, today is a bust. We didn't get a new client, and I know nothing more about Phoebe and her background."

"Look, Suzie, you need to stop poking around in Phoebe's business."

"No. She's our employee. We need to do make sure she isn't a criminal."

"Did she have a rap sheet when you did her background check?"

"No, but—"

"That's good enough for me." When she opens her mouth to argue with me, I raise my hand to stop her. "Think about it, Suzie. Why else would her record only be a year old? What's the most likely explanation? Hint. It's not because she's some mastermind criminal."

She bobs her head as her eyes widen in excitement. "See? I told you she's in WITSEC."

I groan. "No, Suzie. Be realistic. She could be hiding from someone. Someone scary. If she were in WITSEC, they would have given her a complete background."

I may have asked Wally what he knows about WITSEC. I may not want Suzie digging around in Phoebe's past, but I was still curious as all get out. He explained how those in WITSEC have complete backgrounds with no red flags at all. Which means Phoebe is not in WITSEC.

"Fine," she grumbles as she stands. "I'll drop it."

I'm not stupid. I know she'll bring up Phoebe's past again and again. I just hope Suzie's snooping doesn't attract whatever or whoever Phoebe is running from.

Chapter 16

A screwdriver walks into a bar. The bartender says, "Hey, we have a drink named after you!" The screwdriver asks, "You have a drink named Philip?" ~ Text from Hailey to Pops

I SEE THE DOOR to my car is open as I walk toward my parking spot in the garage under our building. What the hell? I quicken my pace. Shit. My car door is definitely hanging open. I search the area, but I don't see anyone else down here.

Once I make I-am-not-going-to-die-with-a-knife-in-the-back-like-a-horror-movie sure I'm alone, I search my car to see if anything is missing. Nothing is out of place. Even my cluttered tray of lip gloss and hand sanitizer looks untouched. I open the glove compartment. Yep, still the same old boring papers as well as a few leftover napkins from fast-food restaurants.

I debate calling the police for approximately thirty seconds. In the end, I decide against it. There's nothing to be seen here. Sure, they may be able to dust for prints but there's no telling if this break-in is connected to the break-ins at my house and business. I start up the engine and head toward the pub.

I growl when I walk into McGraw's Pub and see Aiden surrounded by Pops and my uncles. First, my car and now this.

"What's going on here?" I ask. No one answers. Of course, they don't. I turn on Aiden. "Are you stalking me now or what?"

He leans forward and kisses my forehead. I'm quickly becoming addicted to those forehead kisses. "It's good to see you, too, honey."

I tap my foot. "Is someone going to answer my question?" The uncles look anywhere but at me. I glare at Pops. "I don't get it. First, you don't like him. Then, you do and encourage me to go out with him. And now what? You're pals?" I glare at the uncles. "Did you even do a background check?"

Wally grunts. "What is this? Amateur hour? Of course, we did." He frowns at Aiden. "By the way, we need to talk about your credit rating."

Aiden's brow wrinkles. "My credit rating? I have a good credit rating. I hardly have any debt. I don't even own a credit card."

Wally shakes his head. "You don't build good credit without taking out some loans and having a credit card."

"That makes no sense." I have to agree with Aiden. How does having debt give you a good credit rating? Talk about confusing. "Besides, I plan to get a VA home loan when I decide to buy a place."

The uncles grunt in approval. Of course, they like him. He's a fellow Army vet. I should have known. Now, they're going to be all up in my business trying to push us together.

Pops slides a beer in front of me. "Go ahead and grab a booth, Babycakes. I'll put in an order for hamburgers for you." See? Case in point.

Aiden grabs his own beer with one hand before placing his other hand on the small of my back and pushing me toward a booth. He gets close and whispers, "I like your family."

I snort. He would.

"And? How was your day?" he asks once we're settled in a booth on the opposite side of the room from the uncles.

"Hold up," I tell him before shouting to the uncles. "If you use the bionic ear listening device to eavesdrop, I'll stick mayonnaise in your cream donuts until the end of time."

"You're mean," Wally shouts back, but he does put the listening device away.

"Hey, Aiden," Lenny yells. When Aiden looks his way, he asks, "What happened to the man who hurt Hailey?" When Aiden shrugs, he continues. "Hurt our Hailey and you'll find out."

"Message received."

"I'm sorry. My uncles are a little overprotective."

Aiden chuckles. "A little? How do they even run background checks?"

I don't answer. I'm not telling him about Wally's connections.

"Anyway, you were going to tell me about your day."

I was? Okay, then. I go on to explain about my run-in with Estelle Bostwick.

I barely finish my story before he starts ordering me around. "You are not taking a murder case!"

Oh no, he didn't. No man orders me around. I don't care how hot they are. "You are not telling me what to do!"

"I sure the hell will tell you what to do if you're diving headfirst into danger."

I growl. This is the same excuse I've heard from Pops and the uncles my entire life. It's getting old.

Before I have a chance to give Aiden a piece of my mind, Suzie shouts from the other side of the room. "She already turned the job down. You can stop arguing and start making up now."

Aiden ignores Suzie and pulls my hand close. "I'm serious. Estelle Bostwick is not the innocent socialite wife she pretends to be."

"Wrong thing to say, dude. Now she's curious," Lenny shouts.

I swivel my head to glare at him. He shrugs. "What? Wally said he wouldn't use the listening device. I didn't."

I stand and stomp over to them. I hold out my hand. "Give it to me." No one moves. "Give it to me or I will tell everyone at the bar about the time you all got drunk and decided to—"

"Okay! Okay!" they shout in unison before I can tell the entire bar what a bad idea it is to try and rappel off the U.S. Bank Center.

Lenny shoves the listening device to me. "You're no fun."

"That's what she said!" I say and Barney high-fives me before I walk back to Aiden carrying the device.

"Things are never going to be boring when I'm around you, are they?"

Is he worried about getting bored? This is the second time he's brought it up. "You get used to them."

Pops arrives with two plates loaded down with hamburgers too big to take a bite of and enough French fries to satisfy even my hunger. "No one tells my daughter what to do," he growls at Aiden who raises his hands in surrender.

"And you." Pops points at me. "You aren't taking a murder case. I put up with your investigator business because I know you can take care of yourself, but murders?" He shakes his head. "I'm drawing the line."

I count to twenty in my head as I stand and face Pops. I remind myself committing patricide while in the presence of a cop is a bad idea. "You put up with my investigator business?"

The uncles rush to Pops and pull him away. "Come on, Max. Let the kids enjoy their dinner. Hails already said she wasn't taking the case."

I stalk after them. This is not over. But a hand on my wrist stops me. "Let him go, honey. He's your dad. He's allowed to worry about you."

I collapse in my seat. "Worry about me? Yes. Put up with my business? No."

"I'm sure he didn't mean it how it sounded." Aiden rubs my pulse point with his thumb and my heartbeat starts to beat out of control. Judging by the smirk on his face, he feels it.

My stomach growls and his smirk grows. "Are you ever not hungry?"

"Do we need to have the conversation about me not being a pig again?"

His eyes widen. "No!"

I giggle as I grab my hamburger and take a huge bite.

Two hours later, my stomach is sore from laughing and my cheeks are aching from smiling. I don't think I've had this much fun for a long time. I certainly haven't had this much fun on a date ever. Wait. Is this even a date?

"Yes, Hailey McGraw, this is a date. And now I'm taking you home."

My nipples like his idea. A lot. "I have my car."

"I'll follow you home."

When we arrive at my house, I waste no time grabbing Aiden's hand and hauling him into my place. As soon as we're inside, I throw him onto my couch and climb on top of him. I mold my mouth to his, and he allows me to be in charge for approximately five seconds before taking control.

He growls and shoves his hands into my hair before tilting my head to his liking. He licks into my mouth as if he's tasting a piece of delicious chocolate cake and he can't get enough. I start to grind against him. I feel him harden below me, and it spurs me on to grind harder.

Aiden rips his mouth away from mine to trail his lips down my neck. He nips the spot where my neck connects to my shoulder, and I groan letting my head fall back. His hands slide beneath my shirt and I raise my arms so he can rid me of the thing. It's in my way and I want it gone.

He chuckles. "It's gone." Oh shit. Did I speak out loud? I forget my question when he latches onto my bra-covered nipple and bites down.

"Oh god," I squeak and start grinding faster and faster.

"No, you don't. You're not coming with your pants on."

Oh, goodie. More clothes are coming off. He places his hands on my hips to slow my movements before helping me to my feet. He reaches forward and rips the button of my jeans open and lowers the zipper.

"I'm dying to taste you." I am down with his idea. He lowers me so I'm laying on my back on the sofa. Then, he winks and dives in. At the first lick, I groan and reach back to grab hold of the armrest of the sofa.

His tongue circles my entrance before moving to my clit and nipping it with his teeth. I groan and he shoves two fingers in me as he nips my clit again. I explode. "Oh god!" I shout as I come harder than I've ever come before. I should probably be embarrassed about how quickly he can get me off, but I feel too good to care right now.

When my heart rate returns to normal, I realize Aiden is standing. "Where the hell are you going?" I ask as I watch him adjust the hard manhood in his pants.

"I'm trying to take things slow."

I motion to the pants around my ankles. "What about this situation spells slow?"

He shrugs. "I couldn't resist tasting you."

I have no response. That's the sexiest thing anyone has ever said to me. He reaches down and pulls my pants up my legs. He buttons them and then helps me stand. He keeps a hold of my hand as he walks to the door.

"Make sure you set the alarm and lock the doors." I roll my eyes. The men in my life are going to drive me to drink.

He kisses me and I can taste myself on his lips. Instead of grossing me out, it turns me on. He chuckles and pulls away. "No, you sexy vixen. We're taking things slow."

I pout. "I didn't agree to take things slow."

He kisses the tip of my nose. "Lock up after me."

"Thanks for the reminder. It's been at least a minute since the last time you told me."

"Sleep well, honey."

Chapter 17

What do you call a Private Investigator who is bad at his job? A Defective! ~ Text from Hailey to Suzie

SUZIE SKIPS INTO THE office the next morning. And I do mean hippity-hoppity skips. "Good morning! You won't believe what happened to me this morning."

Nothing ever 'happens' to Suzie. No. She causes chaos and then looks around at the mess she created with this innocent expression on her face like 'What happened?'. Innocent, my ass. You can't call someone a Nazi goat-fucker and then act surprised when he decides to beat the everliving shit out of you.

"What now?"

She halts her skipping to stare at me. "You didn't use your snarky voice to ask." She comes closer and peers into my eyes. Suddenly, her eyes widen, and she claps. "You got laid last night!"

"Phoebe," she shouts. "You owe me ten bucks."

Phoebe rushes in. "Ten dollars for what? Is it someone's birthday?"

"No, I bet Hailey and Aiden would seal the deal last night. I win. You lose." Suzie puts out her hand expecting Phoebe to slap ten bucks into it.

Phoebe's forehead wrinkles. "I never bet with you. And I certainly wouldn't make a bet about when Hailey and Aiden would seal the deal."

"Oh, right. It's the uncles." Suzie whips out her phone. No doubt to call my uncles and Pops and tell them Aiden and I had sex last night. Not happening.

I jump up and rush her. I grab her phone and hold it above my head. "No one is telling anyone I had sex last night."

She grabs my arm and tries to climb me like a tree to reach her phone. I push her away and she goes reeling toward the wall. She catches herself right before she falls to the floor. She sticks out her bottom lip and pouts. "But mama has her eyes on a new fermentation bucket."

"You didn't win the bet. Aiden and I didn't have sex last night," I hiss at her and feel my face heat.

"Oh." Her shoulders drop. "Why not?"

I ignore her and return to my desk. "Don't we have a new client coming in soon?"

My phone dings and – even though I know looking at my phone while Suzie is in the room is the worst idea ever – I can't stop myself from reading the text.

I can still taste you on my lips.

Oh boy. Aiden is a dirty boy. And I like it. I fan my face.

"What happened? Who is the message from?"

Oops. I forgot she was in the room for a second there.

"Let Hailey have her little secret," Phoebe says as she tries to pull Suzie out of my office.

Suzie plants her feet and refuses to budge. "You would know all about having secrets, wouldn't you?"

Phoebe's face turns bright red. Seriously. Her face matches the bottom of her Louboutins. She looks at me with wide eyes.

"Suzie, Suzie, Suzie," I call her name until she looks at me. "Everyone has secrets we don't want everyone to know." She opens her mouth to say who knows what, but I shut her up. "Like the time in junior high when you—"

She screams and rushes me to cover my face with her hands. "No. We don't talk about the Carrie day – ever. You promised."

I pry her hands off of my face. "Well, then, I guess you won't be bugging Phoebe about her secrets any time soon."

She flutters her lashes at me. "But I'm curious."

"You know what they say, curiosity killed the cat." I'm curious as hell, too. But I'm not going to bug Phoebe to reveal her secrets. I have a feeling if we push her too far, she'll run. And not run away for the day to drown herself in ice cream like a normal woman. No, she'll take off, never to be heard from again.

The door to *You Cheat, We Eat* opens and the security alarm buzzes.

"You are literally saved by the bell, my friend," Suzie says to Phoebe.

Phoebe doesn't respond. She backs out of my office and rushes to the filing room as fast as her Louboutin-covered feet can take her, which is surprisingly fast by the way.

Suzie greets the client and ushers him into my office. "This is our private investigator, Hailey McGraw. Hailey, this is ..."

The man steps forward and offers me his hand. "Benjamin."

I shake his hand and try not to cringe when he squeezes my hand to the point of pain. "Benjamin ..."

"Jones," he fills in. If his last name is Jones, then I'm a green alien from Mars. Spoiler alert – Aliens don't exist.

I indicate a chair. "Please, have a seat."

I watch as he sits. The man is one scary looking dude. First of all, he's big. He must be several inches over six-foot and he's as broad as a house. And then there's his face. There's a permanent scowl etched into his forehead and a muscle in his jaw is ticking away. I'm nearly afraid to ask what he could possibly need an investigator for, but Pops didn't raise no chicken.

"How can I help you?"

"I think my wife is cheating on me."

"You're married?" The man is scary as hell. Who would marry him?

He raises an eyebrow at me, and I quickly cover my tracks. "Sorry." I point to his left hand. "But you're not wearing a wedding ring." Good save, Hailey.

He looks at his left hand and grunts. "Anyway, can you tell me how this works? You follow my wife and take pictures?"

"A bit simplistic, but basically, yes. If you suspect your wife is cheating on you, I will investigate her and determine whether she is indeed stepping out on you. There's no need to take pictures if you don't want to." Some clients have no desire to see photographic evidence of their spouse's infidelity. I can't blame them.

"But you can take pictures?"

"Yes, of course."

"What kind of assurance do I have the pictures won't end up on the internet somewhere?"

I bristle. I don't know who this dude is, but I don't appreciate anyone questioning my integrity. I may be a lowly PI who gets paid for outing cheaters, but I do have some standards. "We don't retain any pictures of our clients."

He scowls. "But what do you do with the pictures?"

I force a smile on my face. This guy is rubbing me the wrong way, but I'm an actress. I can pretend I don't want to run away screaming bloody murder from the scary, hand-crushing creepy dude. "Once the pictures have been taken, we make prints and give those to you. We do not keep any copies unless you specifically request we do."

"But you do use a digital camera?"

Duh. It's the twenty-first century. Is there any other type of camera available? Scratch that. There probably is, but I have no idea how to use any device but my trusty Canon EOS. I don't tell him any of this. Instead, I smile and nod. "Yes, of course."

"And what happens to the images on the SD-card? Do you erase those as well?"

"Yes," I lie. Well, it's not a total lie. I do erase the images on the SD-card, although I may not erase them as often as I should. It's not because I'm unorganized like Suzie claims. I simply forget is all.

"And you erase them immediately?" When I hesitate, he explains, "I want to make one-hundred percent sure any indiscreet photographs of my wife do not reach the public sector."

"I completely understand. The SD-card is wiped clean once the client's invoice has been paid."

He leans back in his chair. "And how does billing work? What are your prices?"

I explain how our prices are different based on our different services. Naturally, we don't charge the same amount when the husband gives us detailed information concerning the person they suspect their wife is cheating with. "And invoices should be paid within thirty days," I conclude.

"Then, it's entirely possible pictures of my wife could be on your SD-card for thirty days while you wait for me to pay?"

Talk about getting into the nitty-gritty details. "Yes, but you can pay immediately ensuring the pictures are deleted sooner."

He stands. "I think I understand."

I stand as well. "Please, take some time to think about it and get back to us when you're ready." Some clients need time before committing to a PI trailing their spouse. I get it. It's one thing to suspect your spouse is being unfaithful, it's an entirely other thing to see the proof in black and white.

He starts strolling out of the office. I grab a business card from my desk and chase after him. "Do you want to take a card? In case you decide to hire our services?" What am I doing? I don't want scary dude for a client.

Benjamin halts. "Um, sure." He grabs the card and walks out of the office without saying another word.

"Goodbye," I shout after his retreating figure. I don't mention it was nice meeting him because I'd be lying. Dude was creepy.

"It is me or was Benjamin strange?" Suzie asks as she stares at the door he shut behind him.

"Strange, creepy, spooky, sinister... take your pick." I shrug. "Doesn't matter. I doubt we'll be seeing him again."

"Why not?" Phoebe asks from the door to the filing room.

"He's not ready to commit." It's not unusual. A lot of prospective clients walk away and never become actual clients. It's part of the business.

"You don't think he was lying, do you?"

I give Phoebe my full attention. "What do you mean?"

"Like maybe he was here to gather information about you?"

I wrinkle my nose as I consider her question. "I don't know. He asked a lot of specific questions, but those questions aren't completely unusual. Considering all the weirdos online, I can understand his concern about his wife's pictures ending up on some website."

"He didn't ask any questions about your employees?"

I cross my arms over my chest. The mystery of Phoebe keeps growing and growing. She's giving Suzie a whole bunch of ammunition now. "No, he didn't. And I wouldn't answer his questions if he did. Do you hear me?" I wait for her to nod. "I will never give out any information about you to anyone, client or otherwise."

"Thank you. I cherish my privacy."

Suzie snorts behind me and Phoebe's face pales. I smile to reassure her, but I worry Suzie will not be content until she knows every single thing there is to know about Phoebe.

Chapter 18

What did investigators find in Jeffrey Dahmer's shower? Head & Shoulders ~ Text from Hailey to Pops

"You sure you're up for this?" I ask Phoebe as we exit my car in front of the Grand Hotel. "I could ask Suzie this one time."

She giggles. "You're serious? You would seriously ask Suzie to do this?"

"No." I make a disgusted face. "But I thought it would make you feel better."

"I feel better knowing you can kick someone's ass if needed."

I may have done a demonstration of how to put someone in a chokehold on Suzie. In my defense, she was bugging the crap out of me by hassling Phoebe about her past. My little demonstration then led to a class on how to get out of a chokehold. It was pretty impressive, if I do say so myself.

"Anyway, who's this guy and what's the set-up?"

I fill Phoebe in as we walk to the bar of the hotel. It's nearly the exact same scenario as last week. A guy who gets drinks with his colleagues every Wednesday after work and comes home smelling like a rose garden. Men should really learn to take a shower after they step out on their wives. It's not like hotel rooms don't have showers.

"Vodka martini with Stolichnaya," Andy says as he sets the drink down on the bar in front of Phoebe.

"Dude, we literally walked in the door thirty seconds ago."

Andy doesn't respond to my ribbing. His attention and eyes are glued to Phoebe's cleavage. There is plenty to see. She's wearing a black dress with a V-neck, the V of which dips to her belly button. She is showing a lot of skin. I have no idea how her boobs are staying perky, considering it's impossible to wear a bra with the dress. If Mrs. Yard's husband doesn't go for Phoebe, he's not going to go for any woman.

I make sure Phoebe is comfortable before walking to the reception desk to get a key from Peggy.

"Do you think I could pull off her dress?" Peggy asks as she ogles Phoebe.

"Um." Geez. How do I answer her question? Peggy is a middle-aged woman who hasn't seen the inside of a gym in over a decade. I finally give her an honest answer. "I don't think anyone can pull off that dress but Phoebe." Hell, I couldn't pull it off and I don't need to wear a bra most of the time.

I take the key and walk back to the bar before I can get into a discussion about dresses with Peggy. I wear a dress when I have to. I have zero desire to talk about them. I slip Phoebe the key before settling myself in my dark corner.

I fiddle with my phone as I wait for the action to begin. Aiden and I have been texting back and forth since our bar date two nights ago. Nothing racy since his comment yesterday morning, though, which is probably a good thing because I am way too young to start getting hot flashes.

I look up when I notice movement out of the corner of my eye. Nope, not our guy. Just a couple laughing and enjoying each other's company. I should text Aiden and see what he's up to. The couple comes closer and my anger flares. I don't need to text the rat bastard. I know exactly what – or should I say who – he's doing.

Aiden pulls out a chair for the woman. Of course, she's beautiful. With her blonde hair and dazzling smile, she looks like she was a cheerleader back in the day. She's also perfectly put together. There's not a hair out of place, her make-up looks professionally done, and she's wearing a wraparound dress showing off all her curves.

What the hell is Aiden doing with me if this is the type of woman he usually dates? Well, it's obvious, isn't it? He feels sorry for me. Damn it. I hate pity.

Andy places a beer on the table in front of me with a loud thunk. "What are you doing? I don't drink when I'm working." We've been working together for years. He knows this.

He points to Phoebe sitting at the bar. She widens her eyes and shakes her head at me. "Phoebe sent me over. She said she could see the steam coming out of your ears from the other side of the room."

I'm fine, I mouth back to her. I'm totally not fine, but I'm a professional. I can get the job done.

"Tell her not to worry. I've got her back."

Andy doesn't move. "You sure. You're not acting like the calm, cool, kick-ass PI I know you to be."

I smile. "Thanks for calling me kick-ass. I'm fine." I shoo him away.

As soon as Andy leaves, my gaze returns to Mr. Asshole Cheater and his Too Perfect To Be True date. She's tilting her head back and giggling while reaching forward to touch his hand. If looks could kill, she would be dead right now. Stone. Cold. Dead.

But I'm a skilled private investigator – skilled at sniffing out cheaters anyway – and I know better than to believe everything I see. I need to give Aiden the benefit of the doubt. I pick up my phone and text him.

Hey! Do you want to meet up later at McGraw's?

I watch as he picks up his phone and reads the message. He smiles as he types back.

Sorry, I can't. Working. It's going to be a late night.

Working? Late night? Yeah, right. Looks like he's working it all right. Before I have time to mourn my short relationship with Aiden, a group of men arrive. Mrs. Yard's husband is the leader of the pack. Good. Work will keep my mind off asshole Aiden.

Phoebe swivels in her barstool in the direction of the men, and they freeze. Every single one of them focuses on her, their eyes glued to her chest. I don't know how much she paid for her dress, but it was worth every single penny.

The group becomes unstuck and stampede toward her. All of them vying to talk to her. She laughs and dials up the charm.

She's good. Really good. Within five minutes, Mr. Yard is taking her hand and helping her off the barstool.

I watch as they walk out of the bar. The remaining men in the group gape with their mouths hanging open as they watch Mr. Yard escort Phoebe into the elevator. As soon as they're out of sight, I jump up and rush after them. Andy waves as I rush by. By the time, I walk into the hotel room, Mr. Yard has his hands on the dress and is trying to slide it over her shoulders.

"What the fuck? It doesn't move."

I snap some pictures.

Phoebe giggles. "Of course, not. I can't have it falling off before I'm ready. There's a trick to it."

"Who cares," he says as his hands dive for her breasts. She squeaks and tries to get away from his wandering hands, but he has her pushed up against the wall. There's nowhere for her to go.

I set my camera down and stalk to him. "You'll want to remove your hands now," I order him. There is no time for finesse and frankly, I'm in no mood for finesse tonight.

"Who are you?" He looks me up and down. "You're kind of plain, but I'm down for a threesome."

I cock my arm back. I'm decking this asshole, right here, right now. Phoebe grabs my fist and hangs on. "Don't do it. He's not worth it. He's not the one you're mad at."

"What the fuck is going on?"

"You need to leave," Phoebe orders him. "Before I let her loose on you."

"But we haven't finished."

She frowns. "Sorry, but we were never going to finish."

"This is some bullshit," he shouts before stomping out of the room, making sure to push us out of his way as he moves.

"Asshole," Phoebe says. Her eyes round as if she didn't mean to say the word out loud.

I chuckle. "You can let me go now. I'm not going to chase after him."

"Oh, right." She releases my hand. "I'm sorry. Should I have not said anything about it never happening?"

"It's fine. I already have the pictures. But don't ever mention we're working for the spouse. I don't want to be responsible for some husband beating the crap out of his wife because he finds out she hired us to find proof he's cheating."

Her eyes grow big and round. "Oh god. I never thought of that. I will never say anything of the sort."

"Didn't think you would." I grab my camera from the dresser and put it in my bag. "Ready? Let's blow this popsicle stand."

We're settled in my car before she speaks again. "If you want to talk about it, I'm a good listener. And I won't tell anyone." She shrugs. "I don't have many friends in the city yet anyway."

Ugh. I groan. I was planning on ignoring everything Aiden for the rest of time, not talk about it. "Thanks. But I'm good."

"Okay. The offer stands, though. Whenever."

I nod in thanks, although I have no plans to take her up on her offer.

I'm not one of those women who like to sit around with her girlfriends and bitch about her boyfriends, although Aiden is not now, nor will ever be, my boyfriend. No, I'm the kind of woman who likes to take the emergency bottle of vodka out of the freezer and tell it all her problems. Vodka does not talk back. It doesn't push you to give a man another try. And it certainly never blames you for anything.

Chapter 19

Is there an initiation fee to join the man-hater society? Or do you just have to prove you hate men? ~ Text from Hailey to Suzie

I'M LYING WITH MY head on my desk when Suzie walks in the next morning. I don't look up when I hear the thump of a box hitting the desk, but then an enticing smell hits my nostrils. I open my eyes to see a cake box from my favorite bakery.

"Please tell me there's a chocolate fudge peanut butter cake in there."

"There better be. I stood in line for half an hour to buy it," Suzie says as she sets plates and forks down.

"How did you know?" I certainly didn't tell her Aiden is a cheating McCheaterson.

She motions to Phoebe standing behind her.

"I didn't tell her what happened. Promise. I only said she should bring a treat to the office to cheer you up this morning. You know, like how she brings donuts."

I wave Phoebe's concern away. "It's fine." It's not like Suzie wouldn't have sniffed out the juicy gossip the moment she arrived anyway. "And now we have cake."

"Cake for breakfast!" Suzie sings and then nearly takes my head off with the knife when she waves her hands around in some imitation of dancing.

I grab the knife from her. "Let me."

After I finish plating the cake, Phoebe steps forward and takes a slice. My mouth drops open. Phoebe eating cake? Has the world gone mad?

"Walking on the wild side today?" I ask her when I manage to shut my gaping mouth.

She blushes. "I've never had cake for breakfast. I figure it's time to start crossing things off my bucket list."

I'm on my second slice of cake when Suzie decides she's done with waiting for me to fill her in. "What happened? Was last night's honey pot a disaster?"

"No. Although it's a miracle there wasn't a stampede at the bar considering Phoebe's dress." I take out my phone and show Suzie a picture I took.

Her eyes nearly bug out of her head. "How does it stay up?"

"A lady never reveals her secrets," Phoebe replies.

Suzie stares at Phoebe for a long moment before shrugging. "What happened then?"

"A lady never reveals her secrets," I quip

Suzie shakes her head. "Nope. I'll accept vague answers from Ms. Mysterious over there, but from my best friend? Nope. Try another one."

"I don't want to talk about it."

"You want to talk about why your phone is going bananas then?"

My phone has been blowing up with messages from Aiden all night and morning. I'm ignoring him and my phone like a champ. When it rings, I immediately hit ignore. I am not ready to talk to Mr. I-can't-keep-it-in-my-pants. Of course, Suzie sees Aiden's name and jumps on it.

"Why are you ignoring Aiden's calls? What happened? And why does she know but I don't?" Way to turn my disastrous dating life into the Suzie show.

The alarm dings as the outer door opens. I groan. I don't have any client appointments today and walk-ins are not welcome. All the wives of cheating husbands will have to wait another day for my services.

A smile lights up Suzie's face when she sees who it is. Not a good sign. "Hey, Aiden."

Great. Just what I need. Aiden stomps into the room looking like he's ready to tear the place apart. Nuh-uh. He doesn't get to be the angry one. Being angry is my job today.

I jump to my feet and point to the door. "Get the fuck out!"

"What the hell has crawled up your ass now?"

My eyes widen. How dare he? "Crawled up my ass? You really want to go there?"

"Yeah, I do." He places his hands on my desk and glares at me. "I was worried about you. You have a stalker, and I couldn't reach you. But is there anything wrong? No. You're sitting at your desk being pissed about nothing."

"Pissed about nothing?" I place my hands on my desk and lean forward until I can growl into his face. "You cheating on me is not nothing." Although technically, we never discussed being exclusive. But in my life once you have sex – and oral sex totally counts – you're exclusive. End of.

"I didn't cheat on you."

I snort. "Lie."

"When did I cheat on you? I saw you a few nights ago and since then I've been working my ass off."

"Oh yeah, 'working'. Like you were working last night."

He looks away and swears under his breath. There's all the confirmation I need.

"Get out. Whatever this is…" I wave a finger back and forth between the two of us, "… is over."

"Honey, please let me explain."

"Oh, like you explained last night when I sent you a text and you lied to my fucking face?"

He gulps. "You were there?"

"The Grand Hotel. Where all the cheaters come to cheat."

"It's not what you think."

Snort. Like I haven't heard that one a million times before. "Yeah, right. And you couldn't look me in the eye when I called you out about working last night because the sun was in your face." Spoiler alert – It's raining today.

"I admit it. I lied." Before I get a chance to yell a-ha, he continues, "I wasn't working last night, but I didn't cheat on you. I would never cheat on you."

"Then who were you seeing last night?"

"My ex-girlfriend." His ex-girlfriend? Yeah, right. The woman he was with last night was not an ex anything.

"If you were just seeing your ex, why didn't you tell me?"

"I didn't want you to make a big deal out of it."

Suzie snorts. "How's that working out for you, pal?"

Shit. I didn't realize Suzie was watching this entire confrontation play out. I point a finger at her. "Get out!"

When she doesn't move quick enough, I rush her, push her through the door, and slam it in her face. It won't stop her from eavesdropping – nothing will – but at least she will no longer be an active participant in my humiliation.

"Why were you meeting your ex last night?" I hold up a hand to stop him from answering. "Don't answer. Let me guess. She wanted to talk about getting back together."

"No. Actually, she's having problems with her husband and she wanted my advice."

I raise an eyebrow at him. He can't be this stupid, can he? I wait for him to start squirming, but he doesn't. Guess he is this stupid. "You seriously believe she wanted to talk about her problems with her husband with you, her ex?"

"Yeah. I have no interest in her."

"Dude. I saw you last night. I saw her giggle and do the hair toss." He looks at me like I've lost my mind, so I demonstrate by tossing my hair over my shoulder while batting my eyelashes at him. "And she touched you every chance she got."

He shrugs. "She's an affectionate woman."

He needs to buy a clue. "Let me put it to you this way. How would you feel about me going out with my ex-boyfriend?" I wouldn't. My ex-boyfriends are exes for a reason, but this is a teaching moment.

He growls. "The fuck you will."

I bat my eyelashes again and speak in a deliberately soft voice, "But what if he wanted to meet up to discuss his problems with his wife?"

He snorts. "Yeah, right. He—" He cuts himself off when he finally catches up with what I'm saying. "But Stephanie's not like that."

"Are you forgetting I saw you? I saw exactly what she was like." He frowns but doesn't contradict me. "Let me ask you this, how did she respond when my name came up? If it even came up."

He reaches out to touch me, but I take a step backwards out of his reach. "Of course, your name came up. I told her all about you."

"And I'm sure she was super excited to hear about me." I'm totally being sarcastic. I'd bet my bottom dollar she didn't want to hear one single thing about me and tried changing the topic every time my name came up.

"I can prove to you she doesn't want me." Oh, this should be interesting. "We'll do a double date with the four of us. Me, you, Stephanie and her husband."

What? No! Double dates are the worst. They're an excuse for women to show off their boyfriends. Nothing more, nothing less. I don't get a chance to come up with a lie as to why I don't want to go out on a double date before Aiden has sent a message to Stephanie.

"Good," he says as his phone dings. "We're meeting tomorrow night."

I smirk when I get a brilliant idea. "I'll agree to a double date if this date happens at McGraw's."

Proving he's a total idiot, Aiden agrees. "You've got a deal."

I nearly rub my hands in anticipation. The uncles are going to have a ball with this.

Aiden's phone rings. "Shit. I need to go. Work really is busy. I didn't lie about that." He kisses my forehead and rushes off.

Suzie bursts in my office. "Awesome. Good idea to make sure you met up at McGraw's. Now, how are we going to deal with Stephanie?"

I shrug. "I figure my uncles will be all over it."

"And me." She points to herself. "I'll be there as well."

Normally, I'd tell her in no uncertain terms how she would not be allowed to be anywhere in the same vicinity as my date. In this instance, however, she is most welcome. "Of course. But don't be too obvious with whatever you're going to do."

"Me?" Her eyes widen to comical sizes. "Obvious? Never."

"Whatever."

"I don't have time to stand here and debate with you. I have a background check to run."

I knew I could count on her!

Chapter 20

A minister, a priest and a rabbi walk into a bar. "What is this," asks the bartender, "some kind of joke?" ~ Text from Hailey to Pops

DO YOU PERSONALLY ADHERE *to the Bill Clinton definition of sex?*

I re-read the text from Barney several times before a lightbulb goes off in my head and I realize why he's asking.

"Suzie!" I bellow.

She doesn't come flitting into the room. No, she rolls her desk chair to the doorway and peeks her head around the corner. She's no dummy. She knows I'm mad.

I shake my phone at her. "Did you tell the uncles about Aiden and his magical tongue?"

I should know better than to tell Suzie details I want to keep private. The woman's idea of keeping a secret is only telling a select group of people. I've tried and tried to explain to her what a secret is. Hell, I even bought her a dictionary one year for her birthday. All to no avail.

She shakes her head.

"Then, what's this about?" I stand and walk over to her to show her the text from Barney.

The phone vibrates as she's reading the text. I yank it away. I don't want her seeing any messages from Aiden. But it's just Barney again.

How is oral sex using telekinesis? It's mind-blowing.

I respond with a high-five emoji. "Don't think I can't hear you trying to roll your desk chair out of here," I mumble as I press send.

Suzie widens her eyes. "I thought our discussion was finished."

"Not hardly. You need to stop sharing private details with the uncles."

"But how else am I going to win the bet?"

I growl at her.

"Besides, it's totally normal to share with your family."

"Sure it is. Let's ask our normal employee. Phoebe," I shout. She comes running into my office.

"What is it? Are you okay?"

I wave away her questions to pose one of my own. "Is it normal to share information about your sex life with your family?"

She bites her lip as she formulates a response. "Nothing is normal about your family," she blurts out as her cheeks turn a light shade of pink.

Suzie laughs. "She got you there."

Phoebe looks like she's about to pass out. "I'm sorry. Your family is lovely."

I grin to reassure her. "But they're not normal. Yeah, I think I figured that out when Uncle Wally taught me how to hotwire a car when I was fourteen."

Suzie snorts. "But it was hilarious when you told the teacher in your back-to-school presentation."

"How was I supposed to know not everyone had uncles who teach them how to hotwire a car, shoot a weapon, and override a security system?"

"Now, you're just bragging."

I totally am. My uncles are awesome. But talking about sex with them? Nope. Not going to happen. I'm not an idiot. I know they like to take bets. They are addicted to poker after all. But bets about my sex life? There's only one way to deal with this.

Ask the uncles about their latest bet. I text Pops.

Suzie reads over my shoulder. "You're no fun," she pouts.

The security alarm beeps, and the outer door opens. "Hello!"

"I got this," Suzie says before pivoting to greet our visitor. Phoebe waves and returns to her filing. I thought she would be finished with the filing by now. It's not like we have heaps of documents to file.

"Mrs. Bostwick. How can I help you?" What is Mrs. Bostwick doing back here? I already told her I won't take her case.

"Can I see Ms. McGraw? I don't have an appointment, but maybe she can squeeze me in."

Squeeze her in? If she's trying to butter me up, it's working. "Send her in, Suzie."

Suzie shows Mrs. Bostwick into my office and shuts the door behind her, but not before mouthing *What the hell* at me. I shrug before turning my attention to Mrs. Bostwick.

"What can I do for you today, Mrs. Bostwick?"

"Estelle, please call me Estelle." I nod and wait for her to explain why she's here. And I wait.

"What can I do for you today?" I repeat my question when the silence stretches too long for comfort.

"I was wondering if you'd reconsider taking my case."

Damn. I was worried she was going to say that. "I'm sorry. You need someone specialized in murder investigations."

She pulls two pictures out of her bag and then lays them on my desk. "This is Liam. And this is Sarah." When I don't respond, she continues, "Liam is six years old, and Sarah is four. Liam is a mama's boy. He's shy and hates to be out of my sight. Sarah is the exact opposite. She'd walk to pre-school on her own if I'd let her."

I know what's she's doing. I'd be an idiot not to. But it's not going to work. "They are lovely children."

"Who are now going to grow up without their father. If I get convicted of his murder, they'll lose their mother as well. You don't want my children to grow up with their parents, do you?"

Oh goodie, here comes the guilt trip. Maybe it's because I grew up without a mother for the most part, but guilt trips do not work on me. Ask Suzie. "Of course not. Which is why I recommend you find an investigator who can help you."

I stand. She stares at me for a long moment before standing as well. "Thank you for seeing me."

"Good luck. I'm sure everything will work out in the end."

I walk her out of the office. I breathe a sigh of relief when the door shuts behind her.

Phoebe comes out of the file room. "Why didn't you take her case?"

"I'm not qualified to handle her case."

Her brow wrinkles. "But you are a private investigator, aren't you? You do have the proper qualifications?"

"Yeah, but I don't have any experience with murder cases. She deserves someone who has the right experience to help her out."

"Do you see yourself expanding your practice in the future to include these types of cases?"

"I haven't thought about it. We have enough work dealing with adultery cases and insurance investigations."

I suppose murder investigations would be lucrative, but I didn't become a PI to solve murders. The police need something to do after all. No, I became a PI to help women like Suzie – women who were lied and cheated to. Adding insurance investigations seemed natural. After all, a cheater is a cheater is a cheater, whether cheating on a spouse or an insurance company. Plus – if I'm being totally honest – no one was exactly knocking down my door offering me a job.

I return to my office where I spend an hour calling prospective clients and doing a bit of research for a case I'm working on. I notice the husband of one of my clients mention on social media he's going out to lunch at a restaurant. A restaurant conveniently located next to a hotel. Gotcha! I grab my camera and rush out of the office to see if I can catch him in the act.

When I reach my car, I notice a flyer on the windshield. I hate flyers. I grab the thing, intent on trashing it. Except it's not a flyer. No, it's a picture of Liam and Sarah. Someone is not giving up. My eyes rove the garage in search of Estelle. Sure enough, she's standing behind a car two spots from mine.

"This is not okay." I wave the picture at her before walking her way to return it.

"I'm sorry. I'm desperate."

"I understand." And I do. I would be freaking out if my husband was murdered and the police thought I did it. I can't even imagine. "But I am seriously not qualified. You need to find someone who is."

"But all the investigators I've interviewed were men convinced I'm some type of black widow because Phillip was older than me."

Aha. Now, I know why she's intent on hiring me. She assumes I'll be on her side because I'm a woman. "There must be another female PI you can hire." I know the field is dominated by men, but there are other female PIs besides me.

"But they didn't come recommended like you."

"Okay. How about this? I know a detective. I'll ask him if he can recommend a PI."

She smiles. "Thank you."

"I have conditions." I wait for her nod before continuing. "You will stop pushing me to take your case and hire whoever he recommends."

"If it's a woman."

"No." I shake my head. "Whoever it is."

She takes a deep breath and holds it for a few seconds before agreeing. "Okay."

"Good. Now take this picture, I need to get going. I'm running late."

I call Aiden on my way to the hotel, but he doesn't pick up. I don't leave a message. I'll be seeing him tonight anyway for our double date. My lip curls. I am not looking forward to the double date with an ex who has her eye on my man. Whoa. Hold on. Where did those words *my man* come from? Aiden is not my man. We've gone out on like two dates, one of which wasn't really a date. *But you've liked him forever* some little voice in my head reminds me. I ignore the little voice. It's the same voice that tells me it's okay to have another shot of tequila. Obviously, my little voice is decision-impaired.

Chapter 21

If you're dating someone who doesn't enjoy Star Wars puns... Then you're looking in Alderaan places ~ Text from Suzie to Hailey

"Wow," Aiden says when I open the door. He grabs me by the hips and pulls me close as his eyes travel up and down my body. He bends over and whispers in my ear, "I want to rip your dress off of you and do dirty, dirty things to you."

Goosebumps explode over my body and my female bits quiver. "Yes," I breathe out. "I vote we start now."

He licks the skin under my ear before biting my ear lobe and my female bits jump up and shout *Yippee!* "Later," he says.

"Promise?" My body is melting into his, and I think I've lost control of my legs.

He takes a step back but not before he presses his pelvis to mine to show me exactly how much he wants to do naughty things to me. I shiver. This is going to be one long night.

"That dress. Are you trying to torture me?"

Not exactly, but it's an awesome side effect. The main reason I'm wearing this ridiculous dress is a woman called Stephanie who is not an ex who has marital problems. Nope. She's an ex trying to get in Aiden's pants. I am not letting that happen, even if I have to wear a so-tight-I-can't-breathe strapless tube dress.

Aiden takes my hand and leads me to his SUV. I look at the height and the step. Unless I hike my dress up over my hips and give the neighborhood a free peepshow, there's no way I'm getting in there. "Houston, we have a problem."

"I got you." Aiden reaches around me to open the door and then lifts me up and places me in the seat as if I'm light as a feather. "I can't wait," he murmurs as he leans forward and plants his lips on mine. His tongue seeks entrance and I immediately open to him. I thread my fingers through his hair and pull him as close as possible.

He moans as his hands skim over my body. I want to feel his hands on my skin. This stupid dress is in the way. I grunt in frustration.

Aiden chuckles as he rips his mouth away and places his forehead against mine. He takes a moment to catch his breath. "Later," he promises before kissing my forehead and moving away.

Once we're on our way and I've lassoed my libido into submission, I tell Aiden about my day. "Suzie is driving me crazy."

"As I recall, you two drive each other crazy."

"Wrong. Suzie is bat shit crazy and it rubs off on everyone." He snorts. "Seriously. Listen to what she did now." I swivel in my seat to face him. "She and the uncles started a bet on when you and I will have sex for the first time."

"What?" he barks. The hand on my thigh clenches. Uh oh. Time to backpedal.

"They're always making stupid bets."

"Stupid bets are one thing. Betting on our sex life is another." His voice is all gravely and angry. I know I should be concerned about how angry he is, but my body is screaming *he's so hot when he's protecting our virtue.*

We park on the street near the pub and Aiden jumps out of the car and slams his door. Shit. He is seriously pissed. I need to fix this. "It's only a bet," I plea as he helps me out of the car.

"Not an excuse," he grumbles as he weaves his fingers through mine and starts hauling me inside.

I drag my feet, but I'm no match for a pissed off six-foot-three man on a mission. He pushes his way inside and looks around for a second before his eyes fall upon the uncles sitting in their corner booth.

"I'm sorry," I tell them before Aiden has a chance to speak.

"You are not betting about our sex life." He glares at them. "Do you understand?"

Barney and Sid nod, while Lenny and Wally lift their chins. I can see the corners of Wally's lips turn up. Oh no, they didn't. I yank my hand free of Aiden's and push him out of my way. I plant my hands on the table and lean close to stare daggers at them.

"You weren't betting at all, were you? This was a test, wasn't it?"

Aiden wraps his arm around my waist and pulls me away. "It's fine, honey. I don't mind."

"Well, I do!"

Wally stands and approaches me. He places a hand on my cheek. "Hails, sweetie, we need to make sure the man you end up with is worthy of you."

Suzie arrives and pushes her way in between us. "What's going on here?"

I point my finger at my uncles. "They weren't betting with you! They were testing Aiden."

"But I was planning on using my winnings to pay my bar tab," Suzie pouts.

Lenny snorts. "As if we ever let you pay for your drinks anyway." She deflates because it's the truth. The woman hasn't paid for a drink in the pub since she reached legal drinking age.

"I think your date is here," Lenny says with a chin lift toward the door.

I look over my shoulder to see Stephanie and her husband walk in the door. She's wearing jeans, a blouse with way too many ruffles, and high heels. Did she think McGraw's Pub was a honky-tonk bar? Honestly, I don't know what a honky-tonk bar looks like, but I imagine what she's wearing is how people dress at one.

"This is not over," I hiss at my uncles before grabbing Aiden's hand to lead him away.

"What's the big deal?" he whispers in my ear. "I passed the test."

Men. They're all blockheads, aren't they?

"I don't have time to explain it to you now," I tell him before pasting a big smile on my face to greet my nemesis. "You must be Stephanie." I infuse my voice with enthusiasm I am not feeling.

Stephanie's eyes scan the bar. Her lips turn down in a sneer, but when her attention returns to us, there's a smile on her face. "This place is charming." The way she says charming makes it clear she thinks the place is a dump. Bitch.

Of course, Aiden the total airhead when it comes to his ex, doesn't realize she's being facetious. "It's great, isn't it?"

"I'm Ronald," Stephanie's husband says when she doesn't bother to introduce him.

I reach out to shake his hand. Despite his unfortunate name, he's a decent looking guy. Not as sexy as Aiden, but who is? He's more like the clean-cut boy next door. He's wearing a suit with his tie tucked into his pocket. He grins as he shakes my hand and then shakes Aiden's hand. Aiden is not looking friendly. Probably because Stephanie filled his head with bullshit about her husband which Aiden bought hook, line, and sinker. Did I mention how stupid men can be?

"Shall we grab a booth?" I ask and point to the corner the furthest from my uncles. I forgot to warn them about using the listening device, but they wouldn't listen in on people they don't know, would they? Snort. Who am I kidding?

Once we're settled in the booth, a waitress approaches to take our drink order.

Stephanie's lips purse as she looks at the drinks menu. "I don't think I should order my usual at a pub."

I want to wring her stupid neck, but the waitress isn't fazed. "Pops can make pretty much any drink you can think of." She winks at me.

"I'll have a Bloody Mary. It'll probably be made with a pre-made mix, but what the hell."

Aiden's hand on my shoulder tightens. I'm not about to lash out, though. I'd be playing right into her hands. Nope, I'll simply show her how wrong she is. "Come on." I stand. "Pops makes an awesome Bloody Mary. He will blow your mind."

Stephanie doesn't look happy, but she can't back down now. Ronald steps in. "I'll have one, too. I do love a good Bloody Mary."

I smile at him. What the hell he's doing with man-eater Stephanie is beyond me. I stare at her with my smile firmly in place. She can be a bitch to me all she wants. She's not putting down Pops and his bar. She finally sighs and stands.

I walk to the bar with her dragging her heels behind me. "Two Bloody Marys, Pops."

"Hey, Babycakes."

"You let the bartender call you babycakes?" Stephanie's disgust is plain to hear in her voice.

"Yep. Because this old man is my dad." I jump up to lean over the bar and kiss his cheek.

Stephanie steps closer, and I can tell the moment she gets a look at Pops by her quick inhale of breath. Pops has that effect on a lot of women and some men, too. He ignores her and gets to work on the drinks. First, he pours some celery salt on to a small plate.

"What's he doing?"

Typical. She complains he doesn't know how to make a Bloody Mary when it's actually her who has no clue. "Just wait."

She stays quiet as he rubs a lime wedge along the lips of two pint glasses and then rolls the glasses in the celery salt until the lips are coated. He fills the glasses with ice and sets them aside. When Pops squeezes lemon and lime wedges into a shaker before dropping them in, she swivels on her heels and marches back to the booth. I widen my eyes at Pops who winks before lifting his chin toward the booth.

Shit. I can't leave Stephanie with her man-claws alone with my man. I rush back to the table. I sit next to Aiden and he places his arm around my shoulder and starts to play with my hair. Suddenly I'm happy I spent an hour taming my curls into waves that fall down my back.

"How did you two meet?" Stephanie asks.

"We've known each other since high school," Aiden answers.

"Oh, is this some type of second chance romance thing? Giving your love another try even though you failed the first time." Snarky Stephanie has arrived at the party. I don't remember inviting her.

Aiden chuckles, oblivious to Stephanie's cruel intentions. "Nope. It's taken me a decade to get her to say yes to going out with me."

Oooh, what a good answer. The best.

"How about you, Steph? How long have you and Ronald been married?"

"It's Stephanie, not Steph," she insists. I kind of figured as much, which is why I called her Steph.

Our drinks arrive before she can answer my question. We order our food with the waitress and then Ronald grabs his drink and takes a sip. He sighs. "This is the best damn Bloody Mary I've ever had. Tell Pops he's a genius."

"Pops!" I shout across the bar. "You're a genius."

"You know it, baby girl," he answers without pausing in his task of making more drinks.

"Pops is her father. I'm sure she insisted we come here to help him get some business."

I bite my tongue to stop the giggle ready to erupt. If she's going to make a dig, she should at least make it plausible. I let my eyes rove around the room. The room which is packed as it is every Friday night.

"Does he look like he needs our help," Aiden growls.

Stephanie immediately starts to backpedal. She even has the audacity to reach across the table for Aiden's hand. Lucky for him, he snatches it away before she can touch him.

"I like the place," Ronald says as he places his arm around his wife and tries to pull her close. She shakes him off and puts as much space as possible between them considering they're sitting in a booth.

Our food arrives before she can make another stupid comment. I watch her face as the plates with burgers and fries are placed in front of Ronald, Aiden, and I. She's practically drooling and then a salad is set in front of her and a frown appears on her face. She's the idiot who ordered a salad.

I take a big bite of my hamburger and moan. Carol can make a mean hamburger. Aiden nips my ear. "Do not make that sound in public."

I widen my eyes and bat my eyelashes at him. "Whatever do you mean?"

He growls and grabs my hand to place it in his lap where his manhood is making an appearance. I smirk and bite my lip. "You're deliberately trying to drive me crazy, aren't you?"

I shrug, because saying no would be a lie. He's the one who got all hot and heavy when he picked me up and then told me I had to wait until after our date with his ex-girlfriend. Rookie mistake.

"Please tell me you aren't one of those women who gorge herself on food and then purge," Stephanie says in an obvious attempt to ruin our moment.

Aiden opens his mouth to answer, but before he gets the chance, I speak up. "No, Steph. I eat whatever I want."

"And yet you manage to keep your boyish figure." Oh boy, the claws are out now.

I shrug. "Aiden doesn't seem to mind my figure. In fact, he said—"

Aiden places a hand over my mouth to shut me up and growls, "Enough." He glares at Stephanie. "Stop trying to provoke her." He turns his attention on me. "And you, stop enjoying yourself so much."

My eyes widen. "What? I'm not supposed to enjoy myself?"

Aiden shakes his head at me. "Just eat your burger."

We eat in silence. Well, nearly in silence. Ronald moans and groans as he enjoys his hamburger and Bloody Mary. I think I like him. Too bad he's stuck with Stephanie. When we're finished eating, Stephanie claims she has some prior engagement and drags Ronald, who's looking confused, out of the place.

I'm bummed. I was planning to count how many times I could call her Steph before her head exploded. Aiden kneads my neck with his fingers, and I moan. What was I thinking? I've got way better things to do than tease some bitchy ex-girlfriend.

Chapter 22

How do you make a waterbed more bouncy? Add Spring Water. ~ Text from Barney to Hailey

AIDEN RUBS HIS HAND up and down my thigh as he drives. Each time he reaches the edge of my dress, his fingers toy with the hem before moving back up my thigh. My female bits are going into overdrive telling me to *jump him, jump him now*. I reach over and rub my palm against his hard length. He jumps and the vehicle jerks to the right.

"Don't play with fire," he hisses.

"What if I like the heat?"

"You're trouble," he responds with a shake of his head.

"You're the one who promised to do dirty, dirty things to me." I shiver. I want to do all the dirty things with him.

He yanks his hand away from my thigh. "What's wrong? I was only teasing."

"I think we're being followed."

"What?" I undo my seatbelt and spin around. I kneel on the seat and search the cars behind us. "Which car is it? How do you know?"

He grabs my elbow and tries to force me back in my seat. "Sit down and buckle up. This could be dangerous."

Damn. He's right. Bummer. I turn around and sit in my seat like a good girl. "Can you at least tell me how you know someone's following us?"

"This is not a joke, Hailey."

"I know. It's a teaching moment."

His jaw clenches. "I'm not going to explain to you how you can tell if someone is tailing you."

"Fine." I shrug. "I'll ask the uncles. They've taught me everything I know."

He grunts, which I interpret to mean *whatever*, before turning left.

"Where are you going? My house is the other way."

"I'm not leading whoever it is to your house."

Oh, good thinking. "Are they still following us?"

He nods as his eyes continue to scan the rearview and side mirrors.

"Where are we going?"

"I'll drop you off at the station and see if I can catch this fucker."

"I'm going to miss all the fun," I pout.

"You're going to be safe, which is the only thing that matters."

I want to scream and shout at him that I can handle myself and keep myself safe, but it's impossible to rile myself up enough to start screaming when he says things like I'm the only thing that matters.

He grabs his phone and dials. "I'm coming in hot." I don't listen as he continues his conversation. Instead, I strain my eyes in the side mirror trying to figure out who's following us. All I see are a bunch of headlights. They all look the same to me. I seriously do need to talk to the uncles about how to figure out if I have a tail.

"Okay," Aiden says and pulls my attention away from the headlights. "I'm going to stop in front of the station. An officer will meet you. Stay with him until I can get back to you."

I nod and turn away to look outside so he doesn't see me roll my eyes. What am I a child?

"I need the words."

"I solemnly swear I will stay with the officer like I'm a child in need of adult supervision." Steph the ex isn't the only one who can be snarky.

"You're begging for a spanking, aren't you?"

"You did promise to do all the naughty, naughty things to me," I remind him.

"How do you do it?" Do what? "You can make me smile even when I'm terrified for your safety."

He slows his vehicle down in front of the station. A uniformed police officer is standing at the driveway waiting for me. I open the door and jump out. My door is barely closed before Aiden takes off again.

"I surrender. I am your prisoner." I hold my hands in front of me as if waiting for him to cuff me.

He shakes his head at me. "No wonder Barnes is obsessed with you. Hot little thing with a sense of humor. I may try to steal you away," he says with a wink.

"The hotness is temporary. We had dinner with his ex today. This..." I wave my hand up and down my dress. "...is not normal."

"Yep, totally stealing you away."

He puts a hand on my lower back and directs me toward the entrance to the station. I notice his left hand has a wide band on his third finger. "I think your wife might complain."

"Damn. Forgot about her there for a minute."

I giggle as he opens the door and pushes me inside. He sets me up in an interrogation room with a pile of magazines. Like I'm reading a magazine when I'm in a police station. I stand and move to the open doorway from where I can watch all the comings and goings. There's a large room packed with desks, but there aren't many people lingering around. Probably because it's Friday night and they're all out catching criminals. Maybe? I have no idea.

I'm watching a man drag a woman dressed only in a bra and short shorts through the room while she screams and yells about police brutality when Aiden's face suddenly appears in front of me.

"Enjoying yourself?"

"Kind of?" It comes out sounding like a question. "What answer will not set off your anger?"

He takes my hand and leads me to a desk in the middle of the room where he pulls out the chair before pushing me into it. Then, he kneels in front of me and puts his arms on the armrests, boxing me in. "Now, it's time for you to tell me who's following you."

Is he serious? "Why do you assume the person was following me and not you? You're the badass cop. I'm the lowly PI."

He growls. "You're not a lowly anything and you know it."

I shrug. Now is not the time to have a discussion about my job.

"Tell me who was following you."

"Um, dude, I didn't even realize anyone was following us," I point out. "And seriously, I'm not trying to be a bitch, but why would someone follow me and not you?"

"Hailey, honey, people don't follow cops."

This is news to me. "I have no idea who could have been following me. Like I've pointed out ten gazillion million times before, I take pictures of cheating husbands."

"You also deal with insurance fraud claims. Someone committing a million-dollar fraud scheme definitely has motive to make sure whatever evidence you collect never reaches the insurance company. Have you gotten any new cases lately?"

"Actually, I haven't done any insurance claims recently. I've had a few prospective clients. Some weirdo who wanted me to follow her cat. A man who thinks his wife is cheating. But he never returned, so I assume he decided not to hire me. And then the woman who is accused of murdering her husband."

"And you didn't take her case."

Insert eye roll. "No. I told you I didn't take the case. Not because you ordered me not to, but because I'm not qualified. Although—" Shit. Mrs. Bostwick has been super persistent. But she wouldn't follow me, would she? I also didn't think she'd try to guilt-trip me by placing pictures of her babies on my windshield.

Aiden's finger taps my forehead. "What's going on in there?"

"Ummm..." I wring my hands, not looking forward to the response from Aiden the Overprotective. "Mrs. Bostwick might have stopped by today."

"You didn't change your mind, did you?"

"No, but she tried to guilt-trip me into changing my mind. I showed her the door, but when I went to my car, she was waiting for me."

"She didn't attack you, did she?"

I snort. "Seriously? The woman wouldn't jeopardize her perfect nails. She was waiting at my car with a picture of her kids, trying to make me feel guilty." As if. But her ploy reminds me of another incident. "Although..." Damn. I really don't want to tell Aiden this. "One time when I went to my car last week, the door was open," I say and wait for the explosion.

"What? And you didn't think to tell me?" He growls.

I shrug. "Nothing was taken. I figured I forgot to lock it." I never forget to lock my car but telling him that would be waving a flag in front of an angry bull. His face is already turning red. Can he suffer brain damage from being too angry to remember to breathe?

"Stay here," he orders as he springs to his feet.

"Where are you going?" I shout as I rush after him.

"To see a black widow."

I catch up to him and grab his arm to stop his progress. "You can't. You have no evidence it was her."

"I'm going to have a little chat with her is all. It's what I do."

"Not alone, you don't." I maneuver until I'm standing in front of him, blocking his way. I'm not an idiot. I know he can move me without too much effort. "She won't talk to you, but she will talk to me."

Aiden stares at the ceiling as his nostrils flare. "Fine. But you will follow my directions." I bob my head. "To the letter."

"Come on, let's go." I grab his arm and start dragging him. I don't smile with excitement. At least not until he's looking in the other direction. Then, yeah, a great big 'ol smile bursts across my face.

Chapter 23

How can you tell if your husband is dead? The sex is the same, but you get to use the remote. ~ Text from Hailey to Suzie

"Wait," I shout as Aiden starts driving. "How do you know where we're going?"

He grunts. "Every cop in this city knows where the Bostwick residence is. It's where Phillip Bostwick's body was discovered murdered."

It was? I shiver. How gruesome. And now his widow has to live in the same house? Although, she won't live there long if she's the one who murdered her husband. I know you should never believe a potential client is innocent until you've done some investigating, but I don't believe Estelle is guilty. Why else would she be dead set on hiring an investigator? But what do I know anyway?

My mouth drops open when we arrive at her house, although the word house is a disservice to the place. It's a freaking mansion on the lake. Aiden drives up to the gated entry and rings the bell.

"Hello?"

"Hailey McGraw here to see Mrs. Bostwick." I snort at his use of my name. And he didn't want me to come with.

"Hailey? Are you there?"

I lean across the console and shout into the metal box. "Hi, Estelle. Yes, it's me."

"Please. Come in." There's a click as she hangs up and then the gates start to open.

"I'm glad I'm dressed up and not in my holey jeans," I mutter as we drive down the several-hundred-yards-long driveway. Her driveway is literally larger than my front and back yard combined. I tilt my head as I study the mansion. Holy moly. The place is huge. It even has Greek columns in the front. I bet there's a tennis court and swimming pool somewhere, too. Ah, to be rich.

The door opens and Estelle walks out wearing jeans and a t-shirt. She's barefoot as well. Huh. Not what I expected. Not after the fashion show she's treated me to each time she visited my office.

I reach for the door handle, but Aiden stops me. "You will follow my lead. You hear me?"

"Yes, I hear you. I'm sitting less than a foot away from you. I can hardly claim not to hear you."

"Don't be a smart ass. You know what I mean."

"Yeah, yeah." I salute. "You're the boss."

"Stop being a smart ass."

"Dude. Have you not met me? Smart ass is my middle name." I open the door and shimmy my way out.

Aiden rushes to my side and grasps my hand in a tight grip. Someone needs to chill. Even if Estelle's trying to get away with killing her husband, she's hardly going to kill a cop who shows up at her door to question her. I hope.

"Ooooh." She smiles. "This must be the guy you know."

Aiden raises a brow in my direction. "I'll tell you later," I whisper.

"This is Detective Barnes. He has some questions for you. Can we come in?"

She gestures toward the open front door. "Please."

I step into the hallway and have to remind myself it's not polite to gape like a fish. This is not a hallway, it's an architectural masterpiece. The bifurcated marble staircase is the center showpiece as it rises and then splits off into two smaller flights of stairs going in opposite directions. A crystal chandelier hangs above us, and the walls are decorated with paintings even I can tell are worth more money than I will earn in my entire lifetime.

"Yeah," Estelle comments. "A lot of people have your reaction. Come on, this way please."

I blush at being caught staring and hurry to follow her through the hallway and down a half-set of stairs to the kitchen. This part of the house has a completely different look to it. Although the kitchen has every appliance known to man, it feels lived in. There are no fancy-schmancy paintings on the walls, just comfy looking furniture. She shows us to the kitchen table, which still has the remnants of dinner on it.

"Excuse the mess. I just got the children to bed." She picks up the plates and sets them in the sink.

"Don't you have staff to help you?" I ask before I can stop myself.

"I gave them paid vacation after Phillip died. They need to grieve, and I need time alone with my children." Sounds smart. "Anyway, can I get you a drink? I can make coffee or pour you something stronger if you'd like."

I open my mouth to ask for coffee, but Aiden stops me. "We won't take up too much of your time."

Estelle shrugs. "It's fine. It's not like I have anything else to do on a Friday night other than binge-watch *Stranger Things*."

Aiden doesn't respond to her comment and instead asks, "Were you home all evening?"

"Yes, of course. Where else would I be? I've become a pariah since the accusations against me began."

"Your friends deserted you?" I scowl. People suck.

Aiden reaches under the table to squeeze my thigh. He's not being sexy. Oh no, Mr. Detective is telling me to shut my mouth. "You've been home all evening? You haven't gone out at all?"

"No." She looks to me. "Did something happen?"

"It's no big deal. We were followed."

Her eyes widen. "And you think I followed you?"

I don't. I tilt my head toward Aiden.

"What kind of car do you drive?" he asks.

"Well, we have several. Do you want to see them?"

Aiden nods. We walk to the garage and once again I have to remind myself to not stare like some plebeian. There are ten cars in the garage. Ten! Aiden takes his time examining each and every one. He kneels down to look under the chassis and lays his hands on the hoods to make sure they're cool.

While he does his thing, I apologize to Estelle. "I'm sorry. Someone went into overprotective mode when we were followed."

She smiles, but it doesn't reach her eyes. "I remember those days well. Phillip was the same way. Always thinking men were trying to steal me away." She giggles.

"You really loved him."

"Yeah." She sighs with a dreamy smile on her face. "He was my world. I know the age difference freaked everyone out, but he was only fifteen years older than me. And he was a stone-cold fox, no matter what his age was."

Aiden clears his throat. "I think I've seen enough, Mrs. Bostwick."

"Let me see you out."

Instead of walking through the house, she opens the garage door and leads us to the driveaway where Aiden's SUV awaits.

"I'll send you those recommendations tomorrow," I tell her. She thanks me and waves as Aiden helps me into his vehicle.

"What now?" I ask as he starts the vehicle.

"Now, I take you home and do dirty, dirty things to you."

Oh goodie. I may clap.

He speeds the entire way to my house. Looks like I'm not the only one excited to move on to the sexy portion of our evening. After he parks in my driveaway, he turns to me and growls. "Don't move."

I may be an independent woman, but I'm not ashamed to admit him ordering me around in a growly voice has every single nerve in my body coming to life. He sprints around the front of the car to reach my door. He yanks it open and pulls me into his arms. He doesn't let me down as he walks to my front door.

"I can walk."

"Not letting you out of my arms."

I'm not stupid. I don't complain. Instead, I fish the key out of my purse. He grabs it from me and unlocks the door. When the alarm beeps, he sets me down in front of the panel.

"So much for not letting me go."

"I don't want you to think I'm peeking at your alarm code."

I quickly type in the code and turn around to face him. "Why not? I trust you."

He growls again and picks me up. "Wrong thing to say." He hurries to the bedroom and throws me onto the bed. "Strip. Now. But keep those shoes on. I want to feel the points of them digging into my back as I pound into you."

Yes, please! I reach down and grab the bottom hem of the dress. I roll it up and over my head. Easy peasy.

Aiden's eyes zero in on my naked breasts. "You mean to tell me you haven't been wearing a bra this entire time?"

"The dress has a built-in bra." And lord knows I don't need much support. I reach down to take off my panties, but he stops me.

"Please, allow me." He grasps the panties with two hands and yanks. I hear a rip.

"Hey! I liked those." I don't know why I'm complaining. Ripping my panties off is literally the sexiest thing anyone has ever done to me. If I were still wearing panties, they would be flooded by now.

He lifts the panties up to his nose and inhales. "Mmm… the real thing is even better than my memories."

Did I say ripping my panties was the sexiest thing ever? It's now a tie for him smelling my soaked panties. Whoa! It's getting hot in here.

Aiden reaches behind him and pulls his shirt and t-shirt off in one motion, not bothering to unbutton the shirt. I sit up to watch the show. He winks as he unbuckles his belt and lowers his zipper. I lick my lips as I watch him push his pants down over his muscular thighs. Who knew thighs were sexy? Trust me, they are beyond sexy.

"Why are you still wearing your undies?" I complain.

He smirks as his hands move to his waist. His fingers toy with the waistband and I pout. "Stop teasing me."

"Oh, like you haven't been teasing me the entire night?"

"I wasn't." Okay, maybe I was a little bit. It was fun. Building anticipation for a roll in the sheets with Aiden is now one of my favorite hobbies. I plan to do it again and again.

He pushes the tight boxers down his legs and his hard cock pops out. My eyes widen. I wasn't imagining how big it is. My legs automatically spread as he kneels on the bed and crawls toward me.

Suddenly, he stops. "Shit. Condom."

"I'm clean." The words pop out of my mouth. I don't have sex without a condom. Not unless I'm in a committed relationship. "Never mind. Grab a condom."

"Oh no." He shakes his head. "You offered me the promised land. You can't take it back now. I'm clean, too."

"And I'm on birth control."

He moans. "I've never had sex without a condom before."

"Never ever? Not even with Steph?"

He growls and reaches over to pinch my nipple. I know he's punishing me, but damn, that felt good. I groan as my head falls back and I arch my back.

"You like that, dirty girl?"

When I don't respond, he pinches my other nipple a bit harder. I moan and start to squirm. "Feels good."

He bends over and licks my nipple before biting down hard.

"Oh my god." Tingles spread all over my body. I can feel the smirk on his lips as he kisses his way down my body.

"No." I grab his head and pull him up. "Next time. Later. Whatever. I want you in me. Now."

"I thought I was the one giving orders here," he says as he lines his cock up with my opening. He rubs the head up and down, up and down but doesn't enter me.

I grunt in frustration. "You are such a tease." I pop up and sink my teeth into his shoulder. He groans and slams into me. My mouth falls open as a loud moan escapes me.

"Is this what you wanted?" He grunts out as he slams into me again and again.

"Yeeees," I manage to answer between fighting for breath.

"You feel so good. Nothing has ever felt better." I start to squeeze him as I feel an orgasm barreling down on me. "Yeah, honey, that's it. Squeeze me up tight."

I wrap my legs around him and dig my heels into his back. "Good lord, Hails, you're going to make me come."

That's the idea, I think but I can't speak. Not when my release is hitting me. I shout his name as I come. "Aiden!"

"Hailey," he grunts as he pulses inside of me as his release hits him.

My orgasm goes on and on. When I finally come back to earth, it's to find Aiden collapsed on top of me breathing like he just finished a marathon. "Give me a minute." He huffs. "Need to catch my breath."

"Oh, was that too much work for you? Should I do all the work next time?" I feel him start to harden and lengthen inside of me. "Someone likes my idea."

"Let me clean you up and then we'll explore the rest of our options."

He rolls off me and walks to the attached bathroom. After he returns with a wet washcloth which he uses to clean me with, he fulfills his promise to try other options all night long.

Chapter 24

I shot a man with a paintball gun just to watch him dye ~ Text from Hailey to Suzie

LOVE WILL Out

I WAKE UP TO the unfamiliar – yet extremely nice – feeling of someone's arm wrapped around my middle while I'm snuggled up close to the body belonging to the arm. The naked body. The naked body which brought me more pleasure than I knew what to do with last night. The little voice inside my head, decision impaired as she is, urges me to roll over and get this party started.

My head – the calm, cool, collected part of me – is freaking out, wondering how I'm going to get myself out of this mess. I don't let men I'm dating stay overnight. I also don't have sex with men I'm dating without using a condom. I didn't merely throw caution to the wind last night, I lit it on fire and sent it soaring into the sky.

First things first. Bodily urges need to be dealt with ASAP. I pry the arm from my stomach and slide out of the bed. I have one foot on the ground when a scratchy sexy voice asks, "Where are you sneaking off to?"

I jump and spin around at Aiden's voice. "Bathroom." He chuckles as I run to my attached bathroom to relieve myself.

I screech when I get a look at myself in the mirror. My mascara is smudged, my hair is sticking up in two-thousand different directions, and I have love bites all over my body. I look like a woman who spent the night getting pleasure from her fingers to her toes. True story. And it was awesome. But man, do I look like a mess now.

I'm trying to tame my hair when Aiden knocks and then strolls inside before I can reply.

"Hey! I could have been indecent."

He snorts. "I heard the toilet flush and the faucet turn on."

"Oh." I deflate and return my attention to the mirror and the hair from hell. I watch in the mirror as he struts around. I may have slipped on panties and a tank top sometime in the early morning hours, but Aiden is still as naked as the day he was born. It's glorious. His cock is hard and pointed straight at me. I lick my lips.

Aiden wags his finger at me. "As much as I'd like to spend the day in bed with you, I'm not letting you claim this relationship is only about sex."

Hold up. "Relationship?" Are we in a relationship now? When did this happen? We've been on a few dates. Nothing more.

He stops walking to the toilet and starts prowling toward me. "Yeah, honey. Relationship. Or do you always let men bang you without a condom?"

I narrow my eyes at the word 'bang'. "Do you have to be crude?"

He places his hands on the vanity on either side of me and crowds me. "You didn't mind me saying naughty things to you while I was buried deep inside you last night."

My cheeks set on fire. Why, yes, I did enjoy it. Very, very much. He smirks as he nips my ear before kissing the hot spot behind my ear and licking his way down my neck. I sigh and grab his hips to pull him close. He chuckles before taking a step back.

I pout. "What are you doing?"

"Are we in a relationship?" he asks.

I narrow my eyes. Does he want to have this conversation now? There are much, much better things we could be doing. "Are you using sex as a bartering tool?"

He shrugs.

I huff and cross my arms across my chest. "We've only been on two dates."

He mimics my pose except his biceps pop and look entirely too lickable. "Three," he corrects.

I roll my eyes. "Whatever. Still less than a handful."

"Do I need to remind you of the dog tag I wore the entire time I was enlisted?"

I take the direct hit and launch one of my own. "But we hardly know each other."

"Keep trying. We've known each other for more than a decade and a half."

Now, I'm getting peeved. "You can't seriously claim to have known me in high school." I get all up in his face. "May I remind you of how you didn't recognize me mere weeks ago?"

He growls. "We covered this. You are not going to bring ancient shit up every time we argue."

"Babe." I shake my head. "I don't know what kind of women you've dated before, but this is what we do. We bring up old shit all the time."

"Fine. I'll own my mistake."

My eyes nearly pop out of my head. A man who admits a mistake?

"What?" He challenges. "Didn't think I had it in me?"

I'm done with this conversation. I run my finger down his chest. He stops me before I can get to the goodies. I stick out my lip and pout. "Are you seriously withholding sex until I say you're my boyfriend?"

"Boyfriend, friend with benefits, man, I don't give a shit what you call me as long as I'm the only one in your bed at night."

"Demanding, aren't you?"

"I know what I want, and I'm taking it. I waited too long to have you in my arms to let you slip away now."

"Whoa." I take a step back but run into the vanity. "Waited too long?"

"You're not getting this, are you?" Obviously not. "I've wanted you since junior year when you walked right up to me in the cafeteria and told me I threw like a girl at the previous football game."

Guilty. I did do that. In my defense, Suzie dared me and then spent the entire weekend bawk-bawk-bawking at me until I stomped over to Aiden at lunch and opened my big fat loser mouth to shut her the hell up.

He cradles my face with his hands. "I was too chicken shit to go after what I wanted then. Now, I'm a grown man and I'm not letting anything get in my way including you and your stupid excuses."

I stomp my foot. "My excuses aren't stupid. We don't really know each other."

"Fine. Then, we'll get to know each other while we're a couple. And while we're a couple, you will not date other men."

I should probably tell him I don't date much, and I certainly don't get asked out on dates very often, but he's sexy as all get out when he's all growly with jealousy. I may be a modern hear-me-roar woman, but I still melt when a man makes it obvious he wants me and me alone.

"And you won't be dating other women either," I demand because what's good for the goose is good for the gander.

"I don't care about any other woman but you."

"Including your ex, Stephanie." The taste of the name of the woman who wants to take Aiden away from me feels nasty on my tongue.

"Including Stephanie." He swallows before continuing. "Speaking of her, I should probably apologize."

I snort. "It's fine. I know you were just being a man, aka a complete idiot, who didn't realize his ex is a man-eating shark who wants him back."

He smiles and places his forehead against mine. "Do we have a deal?"

I take a deep breath and stare into his eyes for a long moment. Do we have a deal? Can I really, truly give this whole relationship thing a try? I'm an idiot. What am I questioning myself for? We are talking about the man I've been crushing on for the past fifteen-some-years. I nod.

"Yeah?"

"Y-y-yes." I clear my throat. I am not a scaredy-cat. "Yes."

"Good." He kisses the tip of my nose and steps away. I turn back to the mirror to tame my hair into submission. He slaps my behind. "Now, come on and get dressed. We've got places to go."

Wait. What? "You're serious? We're not going to crawl back into bed and test the bedsprings?"

"Oh, we'll be testing those bedsprings again today. Just not right now."

Which is how I find myself playing paintball with a bunch of overzealous off-duty cops who think it's hilarious to try and take the private investigator out. Actually, there's no trying. They do take me out. I'm covered in paint from my head to my toes. Unfortunately, the paintball place supplies gear for everything from your shoes to your hands and face. But hair? Nope. My hair is now a multitude of colors.

I glare at Aiden as he stalks toward me with a smirk on his face. "You are making this up to me with orgasms."

I hear chuckles from behind me. Crap. We aren't alone out here. Now his whole department heard me demand the man give me orgasms. I'm pretty sure the warmth coming off my face could heat the entire city for the month of December, and it gets effing cold here in December with the wind whipping off the lake.

Aiden throws his arms around me and pulls me close. "You have a deal, Ms. McGraw," he whispers. I shiver and mold my mouth to his.

"Save it for later, unless you want us to see how you make it up to Hailey," someone shouts.

I bury my face in Aiden's chest. The man makes me forget where I am the moment he places his hands on me. "You're paying for that as well," I grumble.

I feel his chest move with his laughter. "I'll open up an account."

Chapter 25

What does one saggy boob say to the other saggy boob? If we don't get some support, people will think we're nuts. ~ Text from Hailey to Suzie

I AM IN THE best mood ever as I walk down the hallway toward the office on Monday. I may even be humming as I open the door. Suzie looks up as I walk in. Her eyes widen and a big 'ol grin takes over her face.

"Someone played hide the cannoli this weekend." She jumps to her feet and rushes to me. She throws her arms around me and starts shaking her booty. Yeah, no. I am not dancing with her to celebrate my weekend of getting down and dirty with Aiden. I may be squealing like a little girl on the inside, but I am not dancing.

When Suzie realizes she can't persuade me to dance, she releases me and throws her arms in the air to do some type of victory dance. She twirls around and promptly slaps me upside the head. Isn't having a klutz for a best friend grand?

"Ow!" I shout, although she couldn't hurt me if she tried. Her puny little arms have like zero muscle development.

"Oops!" She doesn't bother trying to make her apology sound sincere. "How was he? Aiden looks like the kind of man who knows it's all about the motion in the ocean."

I am not giving her details. Nope. No way. "Settle down. We have work to do."

"Um, Hailey, I hate to interrupt, but can I talk to you?"

I nearly startle. I didn't realize Phoebe was here. I cock my head to the side as I study her. She's standing in the middle of the room wringing her hands as she studies the floor. Consider my curiosity piqued.

"Sure, come on in." I motion to my office. When Suzie starts to follow us, I shake my head. She pouts as she collapses in her chair. I don't know what she's pouting about. She's going to eavesdrop at the door anyway.

"Have a seat," I tell Phoebe and point to a chair. Once she's seated, I ask, "What's up?"

She starts wringing her hands again. "I finished with the filing."

I figured as much. "Suzie can get you set up with a check for your services."

"Thank you."

I wait, but she remains silent although it's obvious she's bursting to say something. "Was there something else?"

"Um, yes. I'd like to continue working here."

I blow out a breath. I was afraid she was going to ask me to stay. I know she needs money, but our payroll can't support another full-time employee. "I'm sorry. I don't have any more work for you."

"What if I worked for free?"

I raise an eyebrow. "For free? I was under the impression you need a job."

"Yes, but I've been thinking. I could be your apprentice."

"Apprentice?"

"Yeah." She leans forward as she warms to the idea. "I've noticed there are quite a few cases you don't take. What if I took those? I already looked into getting my license and taking some criminal justice classes at the local college."

"She's right, you know," Suzie shouts from the other side of the door.

"You might as well get your ass in here," I shout back. Although I'm technically the investigator of *You Cheat, We Eat,* Suzie and I are business partners. A decision like hiring someone – even if it's unpaid – to join our firm is a decision we need to make together.

"What do you think?" I ask her when she joins us.

"I agree with Phoebe. There are quite a few cases you don't take."

"I'm not okay with Phoebe taking on murder investigations," I insist when the one case I recently didn't take pops into my head.

"I don't want anything to do murder investigations," Phoebe says. "At least not in the beginning. I'm thinking I could help you with the insurance claims. Suzie said you haven't taken one of those in a while because you've been too busy."

I tilt back in my chair and study her. Never in a million years would I have expected her to say she wants to be a private investigator. Well, damn. I'm stereotyping. Just because she's beautiful doesn't mean she's stupid or can't do the job.

"I have conditions," I finally say.

Suzie claps. "Yeah!"

"I said I have conditions," I remind her.

"Of course, you do," she says with a roll of her eyes. The alarm on the outer door beeps. "I'll start to work on the contract. But for now, you have a visitor." She wiggles her eyebrows leaving no doubt in my mind who walked into the office.

"Come on, Phoebe. Let's leave the lovebirds alone." Phoebe and Suzie hustle out of the room as Aiden strolls in.

"What are you doing here?" Normally, I'd be happy to see him. Hell, my body buzzes with memories of all the delicious things he did to me all weekend. But he's got his cop face on. "Please, don't tell me something bad happened."

"Nothing bad happened." He walks around my desk, grabs my hands, and pulls me to my feet. "Your greeting sucked," he mumbles before slamming his mouth on mine. I moan and his tongue invades my mouth.

"No sex in the office," Suzie yells from the other room.

I pull my mouth away from Aiden and lay my forehead against his chest. "I need an office where Suzie can't hear every single thing happening."

He chuckles. "I agree she's annoying, but I like the idea of you having back-up close in case a client gets out of hand."

"Love you, too, Aiden," Suzie shouts. "And I'm not annoying, merely concerned about cleaning up."

I ignore her. "Anyway, what's up?"

"Have you forgotten about the person following you on Friday night?"

I kind of have. In my defense, he's the one who kept my mind off serious stuff by doing dirty things to me all weekend. "No," I lie. "But what does that have to do with you being here now?"

"We're going through your cases until we figure out who has motive to follow you."

"Dude, I don't need you to protect me."

He growls. "I'm your man, and I will protect you."

"What is this? Early nineteenth-century England? Should I pretend to faint and clutch my bosom?" I glare at him. "Maybe I should give up my job and sit at home doing embroidery while you work?"

He sighs as he stares at the ceiling. I can see his lips move as he counts to ten. When he finishes, he lowers his head and looks at me. "I am not trying to take away your independence. I only want you safe."

I poke him in the chest with my finger. Ouch! Note to self – no poking Aiden's rock-hard chest. I pull my finger away and cross my arms across my chest. "And I will make sure I'm safe. I can take care of myself, you know. I even have the big girl panties to prove it."

He raises an eyebrow. "Oh yeah? Maybe I need to make sure you're wearing your big girl panties."

"Dude! I already told you. No sex in the office." At Suzie's shout, he blushes and takes a step back.

"Suzie Langley, you are a cockblocker!" I yell at her. I wasn't planning on having sex in the office, but would a little foreplay have hurt anyone? No, it would not.

"You two are as crazy as I remember in high school." Aiden chuckles. I open my mouth to remind him he didn't know us in high school. "Nope." He places a finger over my mouth. "I don't want to hear it." Can he read my thoughts now? I narrow my eyes at him. He smirks in response. Oh great, he totally can read my thoughts.

There's a knock on the door. "Hailey," Phoebe shouts. "I have your cases from the past six months here. Can I come in?"

"Fine!" I shout back. When she walks in, I give her the stink eye. For someone who is bound and determined to work with me, she sure took Aiden's side awful quick.

She blushes but keeps on walking, setting the files down on my desk. "No one said you can't figure out who's following you yourself, you know," she says and winks before backing out of the office.

I bite my lip as I contemplate what she said. Damn. She's right. Just because Aiden wants to go through the files with me, doesn't mean he's going to be the one who figures out who's following me. Assuming someone is following me. I'm not completely convinced. After all, it's been weeks since the office and my house were ransacked. And who knows if anyone was actually following us on Friday night? I sure didn't notice anyone.

We spend the next hour going through the cases. When Suzie walks in holding coffees for us, I sigh in relief. My eyes are going cross-eyed from staring at all the reports. I am not the kind of person who can sit in an office all day. Hell, I can barely sit still. Even now my foot is bouncing up and down.

Aiden slams the folder in his hand shut and throws it on top of the pile on my desk. "There's nothing here."

I bite my lip to stop myself from saying I told you so. I hand him his coffee. "See? You're making a mountain out of a molehill."

His nostrils flare. "I did not imagine someone following us from the bar on Friday night."

I raise my hands in surrender. "I didn't say you did." I might have thought it, but I didn't say it. Two points for me and my discretion. "But we can't be sure whoever it was is after me."

Aiden takes a sip of his coffee before sighing. "I'm starting to think you're right."

My mouth drops open. "Did you just say I'm right?"

He smirks. "Smart ass."

I lean forward and whisper, "As I recall, you like my ass."

"Damn straight, I do," he growls as he stands and rounds my desk. He picks me up and sits in the chair, placing me on his lap. "How long do we have before Suzie comes barging in here?" he whispers between placing kisses on my neck. I tilt my head to the side to provide him with better access. "Hailey?"

"Hmm…" Did he say something?

He chuckles before shifting me so I'm straddling him. Now, this is more like it.

"We're going to lunch," Suzie shouts.

"But it's only eleven," I shout back.

Aiden bites my lip. "Don't you dare stop the little cockblocker from leaving us alone."

My eyes widen as I realize why Suzie and Phoebe are going to lunch an hour early. "Oh."

"Exactly." He raises his voice, "Lock the door on your way out."

"You got it, big daddy."

Aiden smiles before lifting me. "Hey! I was comfortable."

"Trust me." He winks before setting me on my desk and pulling me to the edge so my ass is nearly hanging off of it. "I'll make it worth your while."

And he does. Twice.

Chapter 26

How is an umpire like an angry chicken? They both have foul mouths. ~ Text from Barney to Hailey

When I walk into McGraw's Pub that evening to watch the baseball game with the uncles, Suzie and Phoebe are already there. Suzie's singing *Take Me Out to the Ballgame* and Phoebe looks like she'd rather be anywhere but here.

"Welcome to the team," I tell her as I grab a chair next to her.

She stares at Suzie. "I'm thinking I didn't think this through."

I snort. She totally didn't. "Too late. Suzie is like a leech. Once she's got her teeth into you, she doesn't let go."

"What if I get a lighter? I heard those work on leeches."

"And now you know why Suzie has practiced putting her hand in fire since a young age," I quip.

Phoebe laughs. Suzie stops singing and looks at her with her mouth wide open. "You laughed. Like genuinely out loud laughed."

I glare at Suzie. "Stop it. You're embarrassing her."

"Can we talk about something else, please?" Phoebe pleads.

"Sure," Lenny agrees. "How about we talk about you becoming a private investigator? Do you really want to be an investigator?"

"Lenny," I growl. "You're out of line."

"A pretty little thing like her is going to be chewed up and spit out."

I widen my eyes. "What you're saying is I'm not pretty and I'm fat."

I hear a groan behind me. "Don't say another word. Anything you say can be used against you," Aiden says before he bends forward to kiss my hair. "Hi, honey."

"Aahhh, aren't they adorable?" Sid winks and gives me a thumbs-up.

"Yeah, sure, adorable." Suzie snorts. "Adorable is why we ended up having a two-hour lunch today."

My eyes widen at the big mouth, and I kick her underneath the table. "Can you maybe not tell everyone in the entire world every single detail about my sex life?"

"Aha! So, you did have sex in the office!" Suzie shouts and raises her hand to give Sid a high-five.

I ignore her. There is no response to her crazy. "What are you doing here?" I ask Aiden.

He points to his Brewers t-shirt. "Game-night."

"Are you sure you can handle game-night with this crew?" I tilt my head toward Suzie.

"I once arrested a three-hundred-pound naked man covered in oil. I'm good."

"Why was he naked? And covered in oil? And did you touch his ...?" I wiggle my eyes.

Before Aiden can answer, Wally speaks up, "What happens in lock-up, stays in lock-up."

"You are totally telling me the story later," I whisper to Aiden, who nods.

"Grab a chair and join us, boy," Sid orders as he points to an empty chair.

Boy? Aiden is nothing like a boy. Although he does have the stamina of a teenaged boy. Lucky me.

The uncles groan. "What? Did I say that out loud?"

"You did," Aiden says before whispering into my ear, "and thank you."

"What are you drinking?" Pops asks as he walks to our table.

I stand and hug him. "Hi, Pops." There are brackets around his mouth as if he's been frowning all day. "What's wrong?"

"Nothing I can't handle." He glares at his friends.

"What did they do now?"

Pops points to the bar which I hadn't noticed is packed with women dressed in short skirts, high heels, and revealing tops. Uh oh.

Suzie giggles before handing me her phone. The Facebook app is open to the McGraw's Pub page. My eyes widen as I look at the poster with Pops' face on it declaring tonight as Ladies' Night. Pops is smiling and motioning to the camera. Over his jeans are the words – *Come in for a stiff one! It's Ladies Night! All night long.*

Aiden stands. "You want me to get rid of them."

"Nah." Pops shakes his head. "They're all ordering those fancy drinks that cost a bundle." He smiles at Phoebe. "No offense."

"Oh no," I mumble when I see the comments below the poster. *He's single, ladies! Serious relationships only.*

No wonder Pops is pissed. He may be single, but he is not interested in a relationship. I'm not an idiot. I know Pops started taking women up to our apartment above the pub once I moved out. But the occasion is extremely rare. Silly man. He still feels guilty for cheating on a woman who left him nearly two decades ago.

"On top of which, these bozos have been encouraging the ladies, telling them I like it when the woman takes the reins."

I laugh. Pops letting anyone take an ounce of control? Yeah, no.

"Do you need my help behind the bar?"

Aiden grabs my hand before I can walk away. "You have your bartender's license?"

I roll my eyes. "Yes, officer. Would you like to see it?"

"He'd like to see something, all right," Suzie mumbles under her breath. I glare at her before returning my attention to Aiden. I raise a brow and wait for his response.

"Sorry." He drops my hand. "Cop reflex."

"That's the one and only time you're allowed to use being a cop as an excuse," I tell him before bending down to peck his lips. "I'm off to help Pops."

"I don't need your help," he says as we walk back to the bar.

"Of course, you don't," I say. "But if you think I'm going to let the uncles get away with that poster, you are mistaken."

He holds up his hands. "I don't want to know."

I follow him behind the bar and grab an apron and tie it around my waist. "Who's next?" I shout. No one answers me. Of course, they don't. They're licking their lips and tracking Pops with their eyes. Ew. I rap my knuckles on the bar to get their attention. Eyes swivel in my direction. "Who wants to know which men in the bar are single?"

There's practically a stampede to me. Good thing there's an actual bar between me and the crowd of horny women. I lean close and motion for them to lean in as well. "You see the table over there?" I point to where the uncles are now sitting alone. Thank goodness Suzie understood my game plan and moved Aiden out of the danger zone.

"Each one of those men is single." They start to throw questions at me, but I hush them with a raised hand. "Not only are they single, but not one woman has been able to tame them." Women do like a challenge after all. "Except for Sid."

"Which one is Sid?"

I point to the blond god sitting at the end of the booth. "He's been married five times, but he's on the lookout for wife number six."

"Are they wealthy?"

"One of them is." I point to Wally who's glaring at me as if he knows what I'm up to. He probably does, but Barney is sitting at the end of the booth blocking him in and he's not budging.

"Will they buy us drinks?" asks another woman. I look her up and down. I don't know anything about her clothes as I know next to nothing about fashion, but her jewelry is definitely not fake. She looks like she could afford to buy this bar by pawning the rings on her fingers alone. Some women give all women a bad name.

I shrug. "I don't know. Guess you'll have to find out for yourself."

The group studies my uncles for a few seconds before they start running. They push and shove each other in an effort to be the first one to reach the table. Sid and Barney smile as they approach, but Lenny and Wally look like they would prefer to face down an enemy line than a bunch of women.

"You're mean," Aiden says from my side, and I jump in surprise.

"They deserved it," I insist and then start taking orders from the remaining women.

I grab the ingredients for a frozen daiquiri and point to the other side of the bar. "You shouldn't be behind the bar."

He chuckles but moves to the other side of the bar where he leans against the wait station. "Can you grab me a beer when you get a chance?"

I grab a beer from the cooler and hand it to him. "I'll be over as soon as the pressure lets up a little."

Fifteen minutes later, I join Aiden, Suzie, and Phoebe at their table. "Here," I say as I set a new round of beers on the table. "Sorry, Phoebe, we're out of Stolichnaya up here. I wasn't sure if another vodka was acceptable."

"Beer is fine."

"Come here, honey." Aiden grabs my hips and pulls me into the booth next to him. We're touching from hip to foot. My body tingles, and I shiver.

Aiden winks before taking a pull of his beer. His eyes widen with surprise. "This is good." He looks at the label. "Short But Stout. Never heard of it before."

I look at Suzie who shakes her head. "It's new. We started stocking it last week. We're the only bar in Milwaukee to serve it."

"I don't know why," he says as he takes another pull. "It's good. Really sophisticated."

"They don't sell it in stores, but I know the brewer. I can get you a case or two."

"Sounds good."

I look directly at Suzie. "Suze, you got another batch ready yet?"

Her eyes narrow and she does her best glare. Too bad she's too darn cute to pull it off. "What? I don't know why you're shy about your beer. It's awesome."

"You?" Aiden points his beer bottle toward her. "You brew this?"

"What? You don't think a girl can be a brewer?"

He raises his hands. "I would never say anything of the sort. But I'm not sure how you manage to brew beer without harming yourself or burning the place down."

"Well, there was the time—"

"Hey!" Suzie shouts to cut me off before I can tell Aiden about the time the firefighters showed up at her place. "I'm not a complete klutz." She lifts her arm and points her finger at him. As she shakes her finger at him, her arm moves and swipes her beer. It falls and clatters to the floor, shattering into a million pieces.

"Guess you proved him wrong," Phoebe says.

Suzie frowns at her. "I think I liked you better when you were a scared little mouse."

Suzie's teasing, but Phoebe's face falls and she nearly disappears into herself.

"Oh shit, I'm an asshole. I didn't mean it." She grabs Phoebe and pulls her into her arms. She rocks back and forth. "I'm sorry, Pheebs. Please forgive me."

"As long as you never call me Pheebs again, we're good."

I shake my head at Phoebe. Wrong thing to say. Now, Suzie is going to call her Pheebs just to annoy her. Phoebe has a lot to learn about being friends with crazy people.

Aiden places his arm over my shoulders and pulls me close. "Having fun?"

"Yeah." How could I not be having a good time? I've got my girls with me. I tortured my uncles. And the man I've wanted since I've known what the difference between boys and girls is, is sitting right next to me. Things couldn't be more perfect.

Chapter 27

Cop: "Do you have any idea how fast you were going?" Driver: "Isn't it your job to tell me?" ~ Text from Hailey to Aiden

DAMN IT. I JINXED myself. This is what I get for saying everything is perfect. I try to grab the piece of paper off my windshield before Aiden sees me, but the detective misses nothing. He takes the paper from me and opens it. A muscle ticks in his jaw as he reads it. Uh oh.

"Inside. Now. Move it." When I don't move quick enough, he grabs my wrist and pulls me back into the bar we recently vacated.

"What? What is it? What did it say?" I assumed it was another picture of Estelle's kids. Guessing by his response, I was wrong.

He ignores me as he pushes me inside the bar. His eyes travel around the room until he locates the uncles. He jerks his chin, which must be some super-secret caveman language, as they stand as one and move to surround us.

"The office. No window access, the hallway is restricted to personnel, and there's an alarmed emergency exit," Wally says before we start moving as a group.

I can barely see through the mountain of men surrounding me, but I catch Pops' eyes and give him a reassuring smile. Judging by the way his jaw locks, he isn't reassured.

Once we reach the office, the uncles spread out like they're my bodyguards. Lenny takes the emergency exit. Barney is practically glued to my side, and Sid is at the mouth of the hallway.

"Come on, son," Wally says. "Let's check the scene."

Adrian starts to walk away with him. "Hold up. Can I at least see the note that has you acting out a scene from the Bodyguard movie?" Side note – awesome soundtrack but the ending? No. Just no.

"Later," he says without slowing in his tracks.

I huff. "You can't put baby in the corner!" I shout at his back. No response.

"Let him be, Hails. He's trying to protect you," Barney says as he pushes me further into the office and shuts and locks the door. Locking the door? Really? Does he think someone can get past Sid and Lenny? You'd need an army to get past those two.

I flop onto the sofa in Pops' office. "This is completely crazy. Someone left a note on my car. Big whoop."

"Come on, Hails. We taught you better. This is a security threat. You need to take it seriously."

He's right. I know he is, but it doesn't stop me from being a smart ass. I salute him. "Sir. Yes, sir."

He doesn't respond, but I see his lips turn up as he stands in front of the door in guard position. Five minutes later and he hasn't moved an inch. If I didn't see his chest moving up and down, I'd think he was a statute.

Someone raps on the door. Barney raps twice back. Only when the person on the other side of the door raps another five times does he open the door to admit Aiden and Wally. I jump to my feet when I see them.

"What's going on? Did you find anything?"

Aiden pulls me into his arms. He's shaking as he rocks me from side to side.

"I'm okay," I whisper. "Nothing happened."

"What if I hadn't been there?"

I keep my face against his chest to hide my eye roll. My car was parked in a well-lit area, under a streetlight, in fact. I walked outside with a group of friends. I'm armed. And I have taken every form of self-defense in existence. I would have been perfectly fine but try convincing the big lug of that.

Wally clears his throat, and I step out of Aiden's arms. He isn't letting me go anywhere, though. He throws an arm over my shoulders and pulls me close. I don't bother trying to hide my eye roll this time. Sid chuckles as he walks in followed by Lenny and Pops.

Pops tears me from Aiden's arms and wraps me in his arms. "Babycakes, what have you gotten yourself into?"

I pull away from him to give him a glare. "Oh no, you don't. You are not going to blame whatever this is on me."

I switch my glare to Aiden. "I want to know what the note said, and I want to know if you found anything outside." He hesitates for a moment and I get all up in his face. "You are not going to keep me in the dark. I am not some wilting wallflower in need of your protection."

He hands me the note, which is now in a plastic Ziplock bag. *I'm coming for you.* Shit. Shit. Shit. So much for not having a stalker and this not being personal. Someone is definitely after me. But why? It makes no sense. I stare at the note until my hands stop shaking and the fear loosens its hold on me. I can't let my family see any weakness or they'll lock me up and throw away the key. No, thanks.

"I don't get it. We went through practically all my files today and found nothing."

"Maybe this doesn't have to do with your work," Wally suggests. "Maybe it's connected to your private life."

I snort. Private life? What private life? If I'm not working, I'm at this pub hanging with these guys or Suzie. Don't get me wrong. I think my life is pretty awesome. But it isn't exactly filled with drama. Unless you count practical jokes from the uncles drama, which I most definitely do not.

"Try again," is the only thing I say in response to Wally's suggestion.

"There is one difference in your private life." Sid points to Aiden.

"You are not seriously saying Aiden is behind this. What? So he can play the hero? I'm not buying it."

Aiden pulls me close. "I don't think he's implying anything of the sort. I think he's referring to my ex."

I scrunch my nose in disgust at the reminder of Stephanie. She's not my favorite person, but even I have to admit she can't be involved. "Nope. Timeline doesn't fit, assuming the break-ins at my office and house are associated with whoever followed us on Friday and this note."

Someone growls and I look up to see Pops is wearing his angry face. Oops! I may have neglected to tell him about the incident on Friday night. "We will talk about this later, young lady." Oh boy. He's pulling out the big guns calling me young lady.

"I think we can assume all the incidents are related," Aiden says. "Which means I missed something when we went through your files."

I raise an eyebrow. "*You* missed something?"

Sid chuckles. "Ah, young love."

"Until we figure this out, you'll be staying with me," Aiden demands.

I put my hands on my hips and face him. "What part of I'm not a wilting wallflower did you not understand? Shall I get a dictionary to help explain it to you?"

"Smart ass. I know you're not weak or a wallflower or whatever word you want to use. But I also know you're in danger. You shouldn't be alone."

"He's right, you know," Wally has to add his two cents.

"Fine!" I throw my arms in the arm before pointing two fingers at Aiden. "But I won't be staying with you."

Don't get me wrong. I'd love to stay with Aiden. The memory of our sexy times this weekend rears its head and I feel my face flush. Oh yeah, I totally would. But I will not rely on any man. Nope. I may be willing to give this relationship thing with Aiden a try, but I know better than to believe it will ever be permanent. Relationships don't last. Just ask my mom. Oh wait, you can't because I haven't seen or heard from her since I was twelve.

"I'll stay with Pops." My room in his apartment above the bar hasn't changed since I moved out after college. I crash there often enough after a night of tequila-filled fun to know this for a fact.

"Sorry, Pops." I wink at him. "You're going to have to keep it down tonight."

He grunts but doesn't bother to contradict my sass. There's a knock on the door followed by two uniformed police officers walking in the office. The uncles fade away. Seriously, they don't simply walk out of the room. No, they sneak out as if they were never there to begin with. You have to see it to believe it.

"Detective Barnes?" The tall, African American officer steps forward. "You wanted to report an incident?"

Pops approaches me and kisses my head. "I'll get your room set up, Babycakes."

I spend the next thirty minutes answering a gazillion questions from the uniformed police officers. How many times can you say *I don't know* in a conversation? A lot, let me tell you. A lot. They finally leave after making me sign a statement.

We follow them to the front door of the pub and lock up after them. "Well," I say to Aiden. "This is not how I expected the evening to end."

He puts his hands on my hips. "If you had agreed to stay with me, this night could still have a happy ending."

I snort. "Corny."

"Let me walk you to the apartment. Then, I need to get home."

"Babe, you don't need to walk me to the apartment. It's an internal staircase. I'll be fine. Pops is waiting up for me."

He ignores me and grabs my hand. "Where am I going?"

I lead him to the back hallway we were in before. Across the hallway from the office is a door with a keypad. I punch in the code and open the door to a set of stairs. I open my mouth to tell him he can leave me now, but he places a finger on my lips to silence me. Then, he pats my ass in a silent demand to get moving.

The stairs lead to a second-floor landing with another door with a keypad. Aiden raises an eyebrow at the keypad. "Pops wanted double security in case someone saw us punch in the code downstairs."

He nods in approval. "Good thinking."

I punch in the code and open the door. We walk into a small foyer. "Did you need anything before you go?" Hint. Hint. You can leave now.

"Yeah," he says before placing his hand on my neck and drawing me near. "This." His lips descend and melt to mine. I nip his bottom lip and he growls before changing the sweet good-bye kiss into a kiss of possession.

Pops clears his throat from behind me. Busted. I pull away from Aiden's lips and hide my face in his chest. I can feel his silent laughter. Not sure what's funny about this situation. Getting caught making out with your boyfriend is always embarrassing, no matter your age.

Aiden bends down and kisses the top of my head. "Good night, honey. I'll talk to you tomorrow."

"Text me to let me know you made it home safe," I tell him.

He stares at me for a moment before nodding.

"Time for bed," Pops announces after the door closes on Aiden. I wait for him to make a comment about Aiden. Make some kind of biting remark about him. It's his m.o. after all. He never approves of my boyfriends. But he doesn't say anything of the sort, merely pats my shoulder and tells me he put clean sheets on my bed.

Huh. Weird.

Chapter 28

What kind of dog does Dracula have? A bloodhound. ~ Text from Hailey to Aiden

"What happened last night?" Suzie asks as she sets a cup of coffee and a cinnamon twist in front of me. "Pops closed the bar down lickety-split. He promised you'd fill us in today."

He did, did he? Typical man. Leave all the explaining to the woman. "Have a seat."

She squeaks in excitement before backing up to sit in the chair behind her. She squats to sit but completely misses the chair. "Oops!" She says as she glides to the floor. She doesn't try to break her fall. She merely holds up her coffee and donut as she goes down. "I'm okay."

I didn't ask. I wait until she's seated before I tell her what happened.

"Why didn't you stay with Aiden?"

My mouth drops open. "What? Who cares where I slept? Aren't you concerned with my safety or curious who is behind this?"

She rolls her eyes. "You'll figure everything out. You always do. But a boyfriend you're hot and heavy with?" She wiggles her eyebrows. "Not an everyday occurrence."

"I've had boyfriends," I argue.

"But not a boyfriend you've had a crush on since high school," she points out.

I open my mouth to disagree with her, although I'd be lying, and she knows it. I change the topic instead. "What do you think? Who could this stalker weirdo be?"

She shrugs. "No idea. You're not exactly the kind of woman who spurs stalkers. Now, Phoebe, there's a woman I could see having a stalker."

I shake my finger at her. "You promised you'd stop digging into her background."

"Digging into whose background?" Phoebe says as she enters.

"Hey, Phoebe. I didn't know you were here today. I thought we were going to start your internship tomorrow?" Good save, Hailey. I pat myself on the back.

Before Phoebe can call me on my shit, the security alarm beeps, and the outer door opens. A dog barks. I look to Suzie. She looks as confused as me. We stand and walk into the reception area where Aiden stands holding the leash of a chocolate-colored dog.

I immediately stick out my hand. "Hi, sweetie. Who are you?" The dog licks my hand and then bumps my hand with his snout. "Does someone need some lovin'?" I scratch behind his ears. His tongues lolls out. "Aren't you a good boy?"

"Girl, actually," Aiden points out.

I look at the dog's belly to confirm. "Yep, it's a girl."

He chuckles. "You needed to look for yourself?"

"Duh."

I sit cross-legged on the floor and the dog sticks her big head in my lap. "Who's a good girl?" I cuddle her close and kiss the top of her head. "I didn't know you had a dog." Shouldn't I have known if my boyfriend has a dog? Zero points for Hailey on getting to know Aiden.

"I don't."

I look up from my cuddling. "Whose dog is this then?"

"If you get up off the floor, I'll tell you." He holds out his hand.

I look at the dog. "What do you think, girl? Should I get up or stay here and give you cuddles all day?" Her big, brown eyes stare at me as if she's considering my question.

"Come on, honey. Get up. We need to talk."

"If we have to do the 'talk', I'll stay right here with my new best friend."

"Hey!" Suzie grumps from behind me. "You are not replacing me with a dog."

I pick up the dog's head and angle it toward Suzie. "But look at me, I'm soooo cute."

"Darn it. She is adorable." Suzie kneels down to pet her, her foot slides forward and she falls on her ass. "Oomph!"

I giggle. Being best friends with Suzie is like having a full-time clown at your disposal. Always funny, but sometimes scary. Don't laugh. Clowns can be scary. "Twice in one day. Must be some kind of record."

"I wish," she mumbles under her breath before reaching over to pet the dog.

Aiden is done waiting for me to quit playing with the dog. He reaches underneath my arms and hauls me to my feet. "Hi, honey," he whispers before he kisses me. I chase his lips. His kiss was entirely too short. He chuckles. "We need to talk."

"You want to talk here where Suzie is obviously listening in or go to my office where she has to eavesdrop through the door?"

He grabs my hand and walks to my office. Eavesdropping it is! "Lola, come." The dog stands and trots behind us.

Suzie starts humming *Layla* from Eric Clapton. I shake my head. "It's Layla, not Lola, you dork."

"Are you sure?"

"Google is your friend," I tell her as I shut the door.

Aiden points at Lola and tells her to sit. She immediately listens to him. "For not being your dog, she sure is obedient."

"She's the pet of a colleague of mine. Or she was. His wife had triplets and as it happens one of them is allergic to dogs."

My eyes widen. "Oh no. Poor Lola. Have they found a home for her yet?"

"Yep, you."

I must have heard him wrong. "What?"

"She's yours. I claimed her for you."

"Oh my god!" I shout as I clap and jump up and down. Lola joins in with a bark. "I've always wanted a dog."

"I know."

Really? I raise an eyebrow at him. "How do you know?" I'm sure we haven't talked about pets before. To be honest, there hasn't been a whole lot of talking in our 'relationship' that hasn't been about my stalker. Damn. Forgot about stalker dude for a minute there.

"Seriously? Don't you remember those t-shirts you used to wear in high school?"

Face meet palm. Those t-shirts he's referring to were horrid, absolutely horrid. Pops' idea to make up for me not being able to have a dog was to buy me dog paraphernalia. T-shirts, stuffed animals, keychains – you name it, he bought it. Except for an actual dog, of course. He refused to buy me a dog when we lived in an apartment downtown with no green in the vicinity.

I kneel down to give Lola some loving and maybe hide my face, which is probably twenty shades of red by now. "What kind of dog is she?"

"She's a Chesapeake Bay Retriever."

"Sounds expensive."

He ignores me to explain the features of this breed of dog. "They're loyal and energetic and make great guard dogs."

Aha! He didn't buy me a dog because I've always wanted one. He bought me a guard dog. I stand and put my hands on my hips as my eyes narrow. "I don't need a guard dog."

"Dogs are a great deterrent for thieves and other criminals."

He's not even trying to deny he bought me a guard dog. "I can't have a dog anyway. I'm never home."

"And? You own your own business. Look." He points to Lola who is now curled up in the corner of my office. "She can come to the office with you."

"I don't spend much time in the office."

"I'll look after her when you're out of the office," Suzie shouts from the other side of the door.

"You were supposed to pretend not to eavesdrop," I shout back.

"Oh. I guess I missed the secret sign," she says, but I don't hear her back away from the door. Typical.

"See?" Aiden smiles. "All settled."

"No." I shake my head. "I don't accept."

He grabs my wrist and pulls me close. "If you won't stay with me, at least take the dog." His thumb rubs against my inner wrist causing sparks to travel from my wrist through my entire body. He smirks as if he realizes the effect he has on me.

I narrow my eyes at him. "You don't fight fair."

"Never said I did." His eyes flick to my lips before he bends over to mold his lips to mine. I moan and his tongue invades my mouth. I wrap my tongue around his and now it's his turn to moan.

Suzie knocks on the door. "If you two are going to make out, can you let Lola out, so I can play with her?"

"This is why I can't have a dog. Suzie will never get any work done," I point out.

He ignores me. "I also have a buddy who will stop by your house tonight."

I wrinkle my brow. "Why?"

"He's a security specialist. He can check out your security system and see if it needs any upgrades."

Someone is trying to save me again. I don't need anyone to save me. "Did you miss the part where I said I don't need anyone to take care of me?"

"It's not a big deal. You need a good security system."

"I thought the dog was my security system." When Aiden only stares at me in response, I continue, "Besides, Wally set up my security system."

"Wally?" I nod. "Okay, I'll tell my friend he doesn't need to stop by."

"You trust Wally, but you don't trust me?"

"Hailey." He tucks a strand of hair behind my ear. "I trust you. I do. But I don't trust the asshole who put a note on your car last night."

Good point. "Fine, I'll keep the dog."

It's as if Lola can understand what I'm saying. She chuffs before standing and loping toward me. She sticks her big head in between Aiden and me and shakes it back and forth as if she's trying to separate us.

"Maybe this was a bad idea," Aiden grumps.

"No take backs!"

Chapter 29

Would Transformers buy life insurance ... or car insurance? ~ Text from Barney to Hailey

LOLA FOLLOWS ME INTO the office the next day. Since I'm carrying a load of stuff for her to make a home for her at the office, she's off-leash. You'd never know I've only had her a day. She follows along like the awesome pup she is.

"How did your first night with Lola go?" Suzie asks as if she doesn't know.

She and I went on a shopping spree at the pet store last night. We bought Lola everything her little heart could desire. She has multiple beds – two for at home and one for at the office. Plus, several chew toys, a new collar, a new leash, and some stuffed animals to keep her company.

"Come on," I say. "Let's get her bed set up in my office."

"Why your office? Shouldn't she be out here with me, since I'm the one who will be taking care of her most of the time in the office."

"I don't want her to be too near the entrance. What if she runs away?"

"She won't run away," Suzie grumps but follows me into my office. I place Lola's bed in the corner she slept in yesterday. She immediately climbs in, turns in circles for a minute, and then lays down with a mini-growl. I place a toy and stuffed animal in the bed with her before hanging her leash on the door nob.

"She is too cute. I'm glad we went with the pink collar. Now, everyone knows she's a girl dog."

"Has she been spayed?" Phoebe asks from the doorway.

Lola lifts her heads and stands before strolling over to Phoebe. She sniffs Phoebe as she walks around her. Phoebe looks terrified.

"Are you afraid of dogs, Phoebe?" Damn. I should have asked her before I decided to take Lola.

"N-n-nooo. Not really."

Suzie snorts. "Very convincing."

"It's just—" Her voice cuts off when Lola jumps on her back and starts humping her. She's really going at it. Phoebe wobbles and has to catch herself on the wall before she falls to the floor.

"Lola. Stop it!" My voice has no effect. I grab her by the collar and pull her away from Phoebe. She whines and does her darndest to fight me in a bid to return to Phoebe. I drag her to her bed and push her into it. "Sit. Stay." She does as I command, but her attention is glued to Phoebe who is now backing out of my office. "No humping Phoebe." Her whine increases as if she can understand me.

I leave her in the office and close the door behind me. Suzie is bent over laughing her ass off. "You might not like dogs, but they loooove you."

Phoebe's face is bright red.

"Is this a normal reaction?" I ask the room. I may have always wanted a dog, but I don't know much about them except pink collars are for girl dogs and blue collars are for boy dogs.

Phoebe nods. "If a female dog hasn't been spayed, they often ...er ... react this way."

I whip out my phone.

Has Lola been spayed?

Why? Is there a stray dog after her? I'll take care of it.

Um, no. Lola has a thing for Phoebe.

A thing?

She won't stop humping her.

This time it takes a while for Aiden to respond. I tap my foot as I wait for his response.

Should we get her a boy dog?

I am not pimping Lola out! I just want to know if she's spayed.

Hold on. I'll check.

Finally.

No. She's not spayed. I'll set up an appointment at the vet.

I thank him and put my phone away. "Sorry, Phoebe. We'll get Lola spayed. Hopefully, ending her reproductive capabilities will help."

"Oh no. I didn't mean you have to get her spayed. She's a breed. You might want her to have puppies."

"Well, she ain't gonna have puppies humping you," Suzie points out in between snorts of laughter.

I slap her over the head. "Stop it. You're not helping." I indicate my office. "Why don't you go sit in there while Phoebe and I talk out here?"

Today is Phoebe's first day of on-the-job training despite my not feeling anywhere close to being qualified to train anyone. All I do is follow people around until they screw up and then I take pictures as evidence of their screw-ups. The main thing I have going for me is my acting abilities. Majoring in drama was totally not a waste but try convincing Pops of that.

"We have an insurance claim today," I tell Phoebe and hand her the file. "It's a simple case. The woman claims she was blinded in an accident. The insurance company doesn't believe her. They want us to discover the truth."

"What do we do?"

"We follow her." Seriously. It's that simple. And that boring. PI work can be extremely boring, but there's no need to tell Phoebe. She'll discover how monotonous it is for herself soon enough. "Ready?"

Her eyes widen. "Just like that?"

I smirk. "Well, I do have to say good-bye to Lola, but I think you might want to skip that part."

She groans. "I'm never going to hear the end of this, am I?"

"Nope!" Suzie shouts from the other side of the door. Is it wrong to wish my best friend were deaf? Yeah, probably.

After giving Lola a quick rub down, we walk to my car. We climb into the black mid-sized SUV. I program in the target's address and we're off.

As we drive, I decide the time has arrived to tackle some uncomfortable topics. If I don't have to look Phoebe in the eye when I confront her, maybe I won't chicken out. "Phoebe, can I ask you something?" Way not to chicken out, Hailey. You wimp.

"Um, sure."

"Do you plan to dress like you are today when you're a PI?" She's dressed in a pencil skirt and halter blouse. She looks like she's on her way to brunch at the golf course, not a stake-out. On her feet are her ever present high heels. I wonder if her feet are permanently arched when she takes off her shoes like the one and only Barbie doll Pops bought me.

When she doesn't reply, I start babbling. "I don't mean to offend you. You look hot. Obviously. Even the dog can't resist you." I snort as an image of Lola going to town on Phoebe pops into my head. "But you aren't exactly inconspicuous."

"Oh." I hear her let out a breath of air. "I never thought about it. This is how I always dress."

"I'm not saying you have to change, but you might want to think about it. It's going to be hard to follow someone in those shoes."

"Thanks, Hailey. I'll think about it."

I wait until we've driven for a few minutes before I approach awkward conversation topic number two for the day. "There's something else." I clear my throat. "You need a background check in order to sit for the exam to get licensed."

"I'm not a criminal," she's quick to point out.

"I wouldn't let you work with me if I thought you were, but your background is sketchy."

"Sketchy?"

"It only goes back a year."

She's quiet as she digests this information. "Don't worry. I can pass a federal background check."

I'm going to have to trust her on this one. I take another turn before the GPS tells me I've reached my destination. I pull to the curb and study the ranch house.

"Can you confirm this is the correct address where Mrs. Singleton lives?"

Phoebe opens the file and checks the address. "It is."

"And now we wait."

"We're not going to go in there and confront her?"

I shake my head. "Not our job. We were hired to follow her."

My stomach rumbles and I realize I forgot to eat breakfast. I blame Lola for distracting me with her cuteness. No worries. I'm prepared. I reach over and open the glove compartment and grab a protein bar. "You want one?" She shakes her head no. "I usually don't bring drinks as finding somewhere to pee is often a pain in the butt."

"You don't think she'll see us out here and call the police?"

"Nah. The windows are tinted, and most people are oblivious anyway." As was I when Aiden caught the person trailing us last week. Which reminds me I still need to get with Wally and have him teach me how to know when I'm being followed.

"The garage door is opening."

I grab my camera and wait as I watch the door open.

"She can't possibly be driving, can she? She's supposed to be blind," Phoebe whispers as we watch a car back out of the driveway.

"We don't know it's her." I take a few pictures and then wait until the car starts forward, so I can capture a picture of the driver. "Get the file out. There should be a picture."

Phoebe gasps and then shows me the picture.

"It's her all right. Looks like someone won't be getting her insurance payday after all." I hand her my camera. "Here, hold this."

"We're still going to follow her?"

"Yep," I say as I switch on the engine. "We were paid to follow her, so that's what we'll do. Fingers crossed she hits a drive-through because I'm starving."

"You're always hungry."

"True story."

Chapter 30

Why do North Koreans hate jazz music? They don't have Seoul. ~ Text from Hailey to Suzie

WEAR COMFORTABLE SHOES

My brow wrinkles as I read Aiden's text. When don't I wear comfortable shoes? Although…I look at the wedges I had planned on wearing. Cute? Yes. Comfortable? About as comfortable as a sandal with a heel can get. Spoiler alert – Nothing with a heel is classed as comfortable in my book.

Why? Where are we going?

Aiden asked me out on a date tonight, but when I wanted to know where we're going, he refused to tell me. I've been bugging him ever since with no luck.

Wouldn't you like to know

Duh. I wouldn't have asked otherwise.

Be there in thirty minutes

Thirty minutes? What kind of date starts at 4:30 in the afternoon? And why won't he tell me already? I throw the wedges in my closet and search for a pair of comfortable but cute sandals. Snort. Who am I kidding? I don't own comfortable but cute shoes. Phoebe the fashion model would. Hailey the PI, daughter of a bar owner? She owns shitkicker boats and some shoes Suzie forced her to buy.

When Aiden arrives twenty-five minutes later, I'm wearing a pair of tan crop pants, a summery blouse, and sandals. My clothes don't scream romantic date with a sexy cop, but he's the one who told me to wear comfortable shoes.

Aiden's wearing jeans that fit him like a glove and a Henley shirt stretched across his muscles. I lick my lips. "Maybe we can stay in tonight?"

"Nope." He chuckles and grabs my hand to pull me close. He brushes his mouth against mine. I pout. His lips barely touched mine for the briefest hint of a kiss. "Where's Lola?"

"She's with Suzie. I didn't want to leave her alone when I don't know how long I'll be gone." I wink.

"Good. I've been meaning to show you my place." My female bits wake up and scream *Yippee!*

"We're going to your place?" Please, please, say yes.

He shakes his head. "Impatient, aren't you?"

Dying of curiosity is more like it. Notice he doesn't answer my question. My pulse returns to normal and my female bits go back to sleep grumbling about what a tease Aiden is.

Once we're seated in his vehicle, I try again. "Where are we going?"

To my surprise, he gives me a clue. "Look in the back seat."

I glance back and see an old-fashioned wicker picnic basket. "You're taking me on a picnic?"

"Kind of."

I shrug and try to play it cool. "As long as you feed me."

He snorts. "I wouldn't dare not feed you. You're like a reverse Gizmo. Always feed it before midnight or it will spawn Gremlins."

"At least Gizmo was cute."

Aiden parks and grabs the picnic basket. When I step out of the SUV, I see where we are and finally catch on. "Jazz in the Park?" At his nod, I smile. "Not bad, Barnes. Not bad."

"Come on. Let's get some drinks and then we'll go find a place to have our picnic."

He grabs my hand and we walk to the beverage tents. "What do you feel like drinking?"

Does he need to ask? I drag him toward the tent of a local brewery I know has an excellent APA. It's happy hour, so we end up ordering four beers. Then, we walk to the park and look for a good spot to listen to the music from.

Aiden opens the basket and pulls out a red and white checkered picnic blanket.

"I never took you for the traditional sort."

He shrugs and looks at the ground, but I see his cheeks darken. "The lady at the store said this was the best blanket for picnicking."

"The lady at the store?" He nods. "Why, Aiden Barnes, did you buy picnic stuff for our date tonight?"

The color on his cheeks darkens further. "I wanted to do something different than take you to a fancy restaurant. Google said a picnic is romantic."

I giggle. He Googled romantic ideas for a date with me? I throw my arms around him. "I love—" I bite my tongue. I was not going to say I love him. I wasn't. It's way too soon. I've spent more time watching Lola hump Phoebe than I have with him. No, no, no. I can't love him.

"I love it! Thank you," I finally manage to say. Great cover, Hailey. Not noticeable at all. Before he can call me out on my fumble, I start pecking kisses all over his face.

He grabs hold of my cheeks. "You're welcome," he whispers before pressing his mouth to mine. I sigh and open to him. His tongue sneaks in, and I take the opportunity to suck on it. He groans and pulls away. "Let's get this picnic set up before we get arrested for indecent exposure."

I reach down to help him with the blanket, although I'd prefer to rip off his clothes and take my chances with the police. What's the point of dating a cop if you can't break a few laws?

I sit next to him and open the picnic basket to see what food he brought. I gasp when I see the contents. "This is not picnic food."

"What? You don't like barbeque? Your dad made it."

I start pulling out containers. "I thought you'd have sandwiches, some chips, and some potato salad. Maybe fruit for dessert."

"A pulled pork sandwich is still a sandwich," he points out. "And there is potato salad as well as coleslaw."

Why am I arguing about this? I must be an idiot.

"And there's chocolate pudding for dessert." I moan. Chocolate is way better than any fruit salad.

He grabs the plates and silverware embedded in the top of the picnic basket. I start piling food onto my plate. We sit close together and lean against a tree as we eat. The food is super yummy. Of course, it is. It comes from Pops' kitchen.

There's no need to talk as we eat and watch other people arrive. People-watching is one of my favorite things in the world. It's probably why I'm good at my job. Being a PI means spending tons of time watching people, although I don't always enjoy watching what my targets get up to. Can you say blech?

"I'm stuffed," I moan and rub my tummy after we finish the food.

"I told you not to eat a second serving of potato salad."

I gasp. "Are you kidding me? Carol makes her potato salad fresh every day. We can't leave it sitting outside in the sun all evening. It would spoil. Talk about sacrilege."

He chuckles as we pack up our picnic and gather the trash. "You want another beer?" He asks when he stands to go find a waste bin.

"Nah." Between the food I gorged myself on and the two beers I drank, another beer would put me in a food coma and I don't want to waste time in a coma when I'm with him.

When Aiden returns, we lay down on the blanket and stare at the blue sky. "Come here," he says and pulls me until my head is cradled in his shoulder.

My body tingles as it comes into contact with his. I sigh and throw my arm over his waist. This is heaven.

"It sure is."

Oh crap. I said those words out loud. My muscles pull tight and I debate making a run for it. He's fast, but I'm sneaky. I could probably outfox him.

"Calm down. I agree with you," Aiden says and kisses the top of my head.

I force my muscles to relax and cuddle close to him again.

The music starts and we lay there listening to the smooth notes of jazz as we gaze at the sky. I'm not exactly relaxed – not when my entire body is screaming at me to tear off his clothes and lick every single muscle on his body – but I am comfortable.

A jazz rendition of *Just the Way You Are* starts. I sigh. "I love this song." When I was younger, I helped Pops ready the pub every day. He'd dial the music up loud and play hits from the 80s. One of his favorites was Billy Joel.

Aiden stands and holds out his hand. "Will you dance with me, Hailey McGraw?"

I look around. "No one's dancing," I whisper-shout at him.

"Who cares? Live a little. You're not scared, are you?"

I roll my eyes. "Of course not."

I take his hand and he pulls me to my feet and into his arms. We don't dance. Not really. We merely sway to the music. I tuck my face into his chest and inhale his scent. He smells like warm summer days that last forever. And who doesn't love those? Goosebumps explode across my body as my pulse increases and my blood heats.

Aiden places his hands on my hips and pulls me closer. There's not a millimeter of space between us now and I can feel every single hard plane of his body. Looks like I'm not the only one affected by our nearness.

He bends over and whispers into my ear, "I can't wait to take you home with me."

I open my mouth to tease him, but then he nips my ear and I moan instead. He licks the spot behind my ear before dragging his teeth down my neck. My bones are melting. I don't know how I'm managing to remain upright.

"What are you waiting for?" I ask when I finally regain control of my vocal faculties.

He bends down and hands me the picnic basket and blanket. Then, he smirks before throwing me over his shoulder. I screech. "What are you doing?"

"Exactly what I've wanted to do since you said this was heaven. I'm taking you home and showing you what heaven truly is."

Well, when you put it that way.

Chapter 31

What happened when the soldier went to the enemy's bar? He got bombed. ~ Text from Hailey to Pops

When I walk into McGraw's Pub on Saturday night, Suzie is already there sitting with the uncles in their booth. After I greet Pops with a hug and a kiss, I join them.

"It's Saturday night. Why aren't you out with your young man?" asks Sid.

"She probably needs a break. Someone had a hot and heavy date last night." Suzie wiggles her eyebrows and fans her face. I kick her under the table. "Ouch! What?" As if she doesn't know what.

"Is your young man treating you right," Lenny grumbles his question.

I roll my eyes. "Just because I call you uncle, doesn't mean you get to act like an overprotective dad."

"What about me?" Pops asks as he joins our group. "Do I get to act like an overprotective dad?"

"Like I could stop you."

He bends over and kisses my forehead. "I like this one."

"What?" I reach out to place my hand on his forehead. "Are you feeling okay? Someone call an ambulance, Pops has been taken over by an alien."

"I don't think ambulances deal with alien abductions. You should probably call Ghostbusters," Suzie says.

"Call those female Ghostbusters," Sid adds. "The movie may have tanked, but those ladies were f-i-n-e fine."

"What did Amy Winehouse have in common with the Ghostbusters?" Barney doesn't wait for anyone to guess before he supplies the answer. "They both downed spirits."

"Corny," I say as I fist-bump him.

Pops clears his throat. "Enough of the wisecracking. I approve of Aiden."

My mouth drops open. He went from 'like' to 'approve' in less time than it usually takes him to decide what to order for dinner. "You're serious. You approve of my boyfriend?"

"The boyfriend she spent last night bumping uglies with?" Suzie can't keep her mouth shut.

Pops' cheeks darken but he nods. "Yeah, the guy came into the bar to talk to me."

I jump to my feet. "What are you talking about? Aiden came here to talk to you?"

"Settle down, Babycakes. He wanted to explain about how he treated you in high school. Apologize for being such an idiot. How he should have stood up for you then and he regrets it now."

My eyes are about to pop out of my head. "He did what? When?"

"It takes guts to admit you fucked up and own your mistakes. I approve." He kisses my forehead before reaching behind him and placing a burger in front of Wally.

Wally's stomach rumbles. "I thought you girls were going to gab all day," he complains before grabbing his burger and taking a bite. He spits it out and throws it back on the plate. "What the hell?"

Pops laughs. "That'll teach you," he says before sauntering off.

Suzie reaches over and breaks off a piece of the 'burger'. "What is it?" She sniffs before taking a bite. "Mmmm… chocolate."

Wally pushes the plate her way. "You can have it." He stands. "I'm going to the kitchen. Carol won't dare screw with me."

Barney wiggles his eyebrows. "Oh, she'll screw with you all right."

Carol is a great-grandma who's in her early sixties. She's also a total flirt who lives to give the uncles a hard time. I love her.

I look over as the door to the pub opens and Phoebe steps in. She's wearing tight jeans, a blouse, and high heels. Someone took our little talk seriously.

Suzie rubs her eyes. "Is that Phoebe? Or is this annual alien abduction day?"

"There's an annual abduction day?" Barney asks. "Why didn't I know about this? What do we do? Call to schedule an abduction?"

Lenny smacks him over the head. "She was joking. You know there's no such thing as aliens."

Barney raises an eyebrow. "Are you serious? After everything we've seen, aliens is where you draw the line of impossible?"

My attention returns to the uncles who are suddenly looking anywhere but at me. Figures. Whenever they start talking about something intriguing from their 'glory' days and I get interested, they become mutes.

I stand. "Come on, Suze. Let's leave the men to reminisce about their 'glory' days that are way, way behind them."

"Hey! My best days are not behind me," Sid argues. "I've got years of better days ahead of me."

"And several wives left to find," Barney points out.

I motion Phoebe to join us at a table on the other side of the room. We've barely settled in before Pops arrives with two Short But Stout beers and a vodka martini. "Good to see you, Phoebe," he says and kisses her hair.

"Someone's been officially adopted into the McGraw family," Suzie points out.

Phoebe looks around as if we're talking about someone else. "She means you."

She points to herself. "Me? But I'm nobody."

Suzie laughs. "Are you serious? Have you not looked in the mirror for the past thirty-some years?"

"Pops likes you is all," I explain to Phoebe. "Considering you're working for us, it's a good thing."

"Do I call him Pops now? This is very confusing."

Suzie tilts her head and studies Phoebe. "Haven't you ever spent time with a best friend's family?" Phoebe stares at the table as she shakes her head.

"Anyway." I clear my throat. "Let's do a toast to Phoebe starting her internship at *You Cheat, We Eat.*" I raise my bottle.

"To Phoebe," Suzie cheers.

We each take sips of our drinks and then the waitress arrives with a platter of nachos and a plate of vegetables. She places the vegetables in front of Phoebe while I grab the nachos from her.

"Um. Can I try one of those?" Phoebe asks as she studies the cheese-covered sensation known the world over as nachos.

I push the plate toward her. "No need to ask."

Phoebe takes one chip and nibbles on it. Her eyes widen. "Wow. This is delicious." She shoves the rest of the tortilla into her mouth, grabs a plate, and piles it high with nachos.

"Pops! We're going to need another plate of nachos," I shout across the bar.

"I think you were wrong about Pops being possessed by an alien. I think it's Phoebe who's been possessed. Ghostbusters is only a call away."

I shoulder-check her. "Stop it. Phoebe's trying new things. It's awesome."

While we eat, we discuss Phoebe's position and how we're going to fulfill it. Suzie and I have never hired anyone before and are feeling our way as we go.

As soon as the nachos are eaten, the vegetables remained untouched today, Suzie zeroes in on me. "I think I've been patient enough."

I raise my eyebrow. Really? This woman may be my best friend, but she'd rather put sugar in her beer than be patient. "What do you think, Phoebe? Has our Suzie been patient?"

She holds up her hands and moves back in her seat as far away from us as possible while sitting in the same booth. "Oh no. Don't put me in the middle of the two of you."

"Come on," Suzie whines. "You haven't told us about your date with Aiden. I want all the deets."

"I am not giving you a blow by blow playback of our sex life," I hiss at her.

"I didn't mean sex, although I'm ready for any sharing you want to do. I want to hear how you're doing with your boyfriend being the man you've panted after your entire life."

I bristle. "I haven't panted after Aiden my entire life."

She ignores my denial. "You've always kept your boyfriends at arm's length because you were holding out hope for Aiden. Now you have the man you've always wanted, you can't keep him at arm's length."

I frown. "I haven't always kept my boyfriends at arm's length."

Suzie looks to Phoebe. "She totally has."

Phoebe shrugs. "Maybe she has a reason."

Oh, I have a reason all right. A huge mother-shaped reason.

Suzie waves her hands and knocks over her beer. At least it doesn't shatter into a million pieces on the floor. She doesn't even blink an eye as she rights the bottle. "Yeah, yeah, yeah. Her mother abandoned her and now she has commitment issues. Yada yada yada." She yawns as if my mother issues are no big deal.

I shoot daggers at her. "How dare you? Did your mother leave you when you were twelve years old never to be heard of again? She doesn't call. She doesn't send birthday cards. She could be dead for all I know."

"Good."

My eyes widen. "How could you wish her dead?"

"Because then maybe you'd finally get over your commitment issues and give Aiden a real chance."

"I am giving Aiden a chance. I'm not holding back from him." I totally am.

She rolls her eyes. "I'm not talking about holding sex back from him. I'm talking about emotionally holding back." She leans forward and gets all up in my face. "Have you told him you love him yet?"

"What?" I hold my hands up and arch away from her. "I don't love him. Sure, I might have almost told him I love him yesterday, but it was a slip of the tongue. Nothing more." Even I don't believe the words coming out of my mouth.

Suzie claps and squeals. "I knew it! You do love him."

"I don't love him," I deny. "Besides, my feelings – if I had any – would change nothing. He could still leave me at any moment."

She grabs my head and yanks it to the side forcing me to look at the bar counter. "Do you see Pops over there?" I open my mouth to answer, but she shuts me up. "Quiet. The adults are talking now." I zip my lips. "Has he ever abandoned you? No. He's been here every single day. Who came to all those silly plays you did in high school? He did. Who helped you pay for college to study drama even though he thought it was a bad idea? He did. Who helped nurse you back to health when you had a case of pneumonia from standing outside in the rain to get 'in character'? He did." She drops her hands. "Need I say more?"

I shake my head. No, I understand what she's getting at, but getting rid of old fears is not easy. But maybe – just maybe – I should at least think about it.

Chapter 32

What did the burglar say when asked why he kicked in his own door? I'm working from home. ~ Text from Hailey to Aiden

A BEEP WAKES ME from a dead sleep. Who's the jerk calling me on a Sunday morning? I roll over and cover my head with a pillow. If I ignore my phone, it will stop – eventually. Lola growls and stands from her bed to walk to my side. She bumps my arm with her wet snout. Ew. I push her away. "Go back to sleep." She refuses to budge, and her growl grows louder.

Shit. My phone isn't beeping. The security system is going off, warning me of an intruder. Shit. Shit. Shit. I jump out of bed and immediately regret it when the room tilts. Lola presses against my leg to steady me. I pet her head. "Good girl."

Lucky for me, I'm still wearing last night's clothes. Dealing with an intruder while half-naked is not on my bucket list. I grab my phone from the charger on my bedside table and creep toward my bedroom door, Lola following me. I press my ear against the wall to hear if anyone is inside the house or if they ran off when the alarm was triggered. Fingers crossed for running off.

All's quiet. I exhale. I'll switch off the alarm and then I can get back to bed where I should be now. Before I can take a step, I hear a creak. The same creak the floor makes when you step on the spot at the entrance to my hallway.

I don't think. I sprint to the attached bathroom with Lola hot on my heels. I push the door shut as quietly as possible and lock it. I'm not under any illusions the knob lock will keep anyone out, but it's better than nothing. I need a weapon. Damn it. Why didn't I grab my 9 mm from the drawer in my nightstand?

My eyes search the room for weapons as I lean against the door to catch my breath. Hair spray? It's worth a shot. If I spray the intruder in the eyes, it might buy me enough time to run away. If not, I need something hard to smack him with. But what? A shampoo bottle? No. I shake my head and my eyes land on my bathtub tray. It's not much, but if I put enough force behind it, it may be able to daze whoever thinks Sunday morning is an all right time to break into my house. Hint – no time is an all right time to break in.

I stand in front of the closed door with the hairspray in one hand and the tray on the vanity next to me. Lola pushes and nudges me until she's standing in front of me. She tries to push me back away from the door. I pat her head but refuse to move. Such a good doggy. If we get out of this, I am totally buying her every doggy treat in existence.

My phone beeps with an incoming message. The sound is practically an announcement to the intruder *Here I am! Come and get me!* I freeze. Why the hell didn't I put my phone on silent when I went to bed? Probably for the same reason I'm wearing the clothes from last night. One word – beer.

"I know you're hiding in the bathroom," a male voice shouts as his steps come closer to the door.

I don't respond.

"Why don't you come out and we can talk? I don't want to hurt you. I only need something from you."

Sure. I totally believe him. Not. I refuse to think about what he 'needs' from me.

Instead, my mind moves to Aiden. I wish he was here. I wish the man I love was here. Holy moly. The man I love? Do I love Aiden? Stupid question. I do love Aiden. I don't know why I've been fighting my feelings. Life's too short to hold back. And now I'm going to die in my bathroom with my dog for company. Lola whines as if she can understand what I'm thinking.

"Sorry, sweet girl, I love you," I whisper as I pat her head. But I'd rather spend my dying moments with Aiden. She huffs and turns back around to stare down the door as if she's disappointed in me.

"No one's coming to save you. You might as well come out here and talk to me." The voice sounds familiar, but I can't quite place it. Maybe I should talk to him. Figure out who is he. I might not survive, but I can make a note on my phone for the homicide detectives.

Morbid, much, Hailey? I stiffen my spine. I am getting out of here. *Come on, Hailey, you can do this.* Talk to the guy and buy some time for the police to arrive.

"Who are you?" My voice shakes. I clear my throat and try again. "What do you want?"

"Why don't you come out here and we can talk?"

"Why don't you tell me who you are and then I'll come out there?" Don't worry. I'm not a total idiot. He'll have to drag me kicking and screaming out of this bathroom. Lola is now growling and scratching at the door. Maybe she'll bite him. Serves him right.

"Tell me where your camera is, and I'll leave you alone."

My camera? What does he want with my camera? Don't tell me this is some disgruntled husband of a client who got caught cheating. I'll never hear the end of it from Aiden. I bite my lip as I deliberate. Should I tell him where my camera is? Will he really leave if I give it to him?

"Why do you want my camera?"

"None of your business. Tell me where it is, or I'll break this door down."

His voice is loud and demanding. Uh oh. Someone's getting mad. This is not good. I take a step away from the door as Lola's growling changes to barking.

I open my mouth to tell him where the camera is. At the very least, I can try and sneak out of the house with Lola while he digs through my office. I hear a grunt and then a scuffle. I place my ear against the door to listen.

"Milwaukee Police. You're under arrest." I hear sounds of flesh on flesh. Oh please, don't shoot someone in my house. I have no idea how to get out coffee stains, blood stains are beyond my laundry capabilities.

"Ms. McGraw? The intruder has been restrained. It's safe to come out now."

"How do I know you're who you say you are?"

"Aiden said you'd say that." Snort. His words prove nothing. "Is Lola in there with you?"

At the sound of her name, Lola barks a greeting and starts scratching at the door.

"Call Aiden. Tell him Officer White is here and you need to verify his identity."

"No need to call Aiden. I'm here."

At Aiden's voice, I push Lola out of the way and unlock the door. I fly to him and wrap my arms around him smacking him on the side of the head with the hairspray bottle. Oops. I forgot I was carrying it. I drop it and cling to him.

Aiden enfolds me in his arms. He squeezes tight, but I don't care. "Shit. You scared me. I knew I shouldn't have left you alone."

I bend away from him and glare. "No macho man crap. I'm not in the mood."

He nods before pulling me close again. I snuggle into his arms for a moment. "Wait. Where's Lola? Is she okay?"

Aiden chuckles before spinning me around. Lola is on her back getting belly rubs from an African-American police officer.

"My dog is a total slut."

"Remember the colleague who had to give up Lola?" I nod. "You're looking at him."

I rush the guy and tackle him. He falls on his butt and Lola attacks us both with kisses. "Thank you for saving me. And thank you for Lola." Lola hears her name and dials up the volume on her kiss attack. I push her big head away. "Someone needs to brush her teeth."

"Come on." Aiden holds out his hand. "We need to take your statement."

Oh, yeah. I was trying to forget all about creepy intruder guy. He helps me to my feet.

"Who was the guy anyway? His voice sounded familiar, but I couldn't place him."

Aiden freezes. "His voice sounded familiar?"

"Yeah."

"Do you think you'd recognize him?"

I shrug. "Maybe."

"Come on." He drags me through my house and outside where the police are pushing someone into the back of a patrol car. Aiden lets out a whistle and they stop. The man they are arresting looks my way and I gasp.

"I do know him. He came into my office claiming his wife is cheating on him."

Aiden puts an arm around me and pulls me close. "Do you remember his name?"

I tap my chin as I try to remember. "Benjamin something. I can look in my agenda. As soon as I remember where I put my phone." I snap my fingers. "It's in the bathroom."

Once I retrieve my phone and look through my calendar, I fill Aiden in. "His name is Benjamin Jones, but I'm pretty sure he used a fake name." I think back to the appointment. I remember he was creepy and scary. And he asked a ton of questions. Well, shit.

"What is it? What do you remember?"

"What a total and utter idiot I am. *Benjamin* asked question after question on how I operate, and I told him. I told him all about how we didn't save pictures. My camera!" I run off to retrieve my camera. When I return, I hand it to him. "When we were talking while I was hiding in the bathroom—"

Aiden stops me with a growl. I shush him with a glare.

"He asked for my camera. He must think I took a picture of something I shouldn't have. He's definitely not the husband of a client. I'd recognize him if he were."

Aiden takes the camera and places it in an evidence bag. Shit. That's going to cost me. He kisses my forehead. "Don't worry. I'll have it back to you as soon as possible."

"Detective Barnes!" One of the uniformed officers shouts. "We're all set here."

"I'll meet you down at the station."

I grab Aiden's hand. "I'm going with you."

He stares at me for a minute before nodding. "You will follow my orders and not go running off on your own."

I shiver. "Yes, sir. Whatever you say, sir."

He smirks. "Watch the attitude, McGraw, or I'll have to teach you a lesson."

I lick my lips. Yes, please.

Chapter 33

If the Energizer Bunny were arrested, would he be charged with battery? ~ Text from Hailey to Suzie

I GRAB MY PURSE and keys and walk to the door with Aiden. Lola follows us. "No, sweet girl, you can't come with." She whines and stares at me with her big brown puppy eyes. Those should be classified as weapons and made illegal.

Aiden grins. "It's fine. She can come with."

"To the police station?"

He shrugs. "She's a witness as well."

"Not sure what her witness statement is going to say besides *woof, feed me snacks*, but whatever."

We leave the house and I lock up while Aiden walks around his SUV and opens the back hatch. Lola jumps in, straight into a crate. "When did you get a dog crate?"

"Figured I'd need it if we're going to be carting Lola around."

I raise my eyebrows. "Awful presumptuous of you."

"Do I need to explain what a relationship is again?" He doesn't wait for me to answer before herding me to the passenger seat. "Come on. We need to get going."

"What do you think Benjamin Jones wanted?" I ask him once we're on our way.

His hands tighten on the wheel and a muscle ticks in his jaw. "I don't know, but I will find out."

Okay then. Moving on. "What did you do last night?"

He doesn't bother responding. Nope, he hits the gas pedal and hightails it to the police station. Good thing it's o' dark thirty and no cars are out and about because someone thinks stop signs and red lights are merely advisory. I like speed as much as the next girl, but when he flies through a red light, I decide it's time to grab the oh-shit bar and start praying for a safe delivery.

"We're here," Aiden announces. I open the eyes I didn't realize I'd closed and huff out a relieved breath. "Come on, I'll get you set up someplace safe while I deal with Mr. Jones."

The menacing way he growls Jones' name makes me super duper happy my name is not Jones. Someone is in trouble. Big time.

Aiden leads Lola and me to an interrogation room. "Someone will be in to take your statement." He kisses my forehead and he's gone. Lola cries and lays down in front of the door with her head in her paws. Such a big baby.

Fifteen minutes pass before a female uniformed officer comes in to take my statement. Officer Green asks me ten-thousand

and one questions. I tell her the same story I told Aiden and then she leaves to type it up. Lola and I are left alone again.

"Honey." Someone shakes my shoulder.

"Ten more minutes," I mumble.

Suddenly, I'm airborne. What the...? I open my eyes to discover Aiden has gathered me in his arms. "What? Huh?" I blink my eyes until my vision clears and I remember where I'm at. "Put me down," I hiss. I don't want to be carried around a police station!

Aiden doesn't argue and sets me down. "Come on." He grabs my hand. "Let's get you and Lola home."

I refuse to move. "Nuh-uh. First, tell me why scary dude was in my house. What was he after? Was it my camera?"

He sighs and releases my hand to run a hand over his face. "Benjamin Jones is actually Bones Jessup."

"Bones? Someone's momma didn't like him very much." I deliberately make light of the name. In reality, it scares the pants off of me. Someone named Bones was after me? Yeah, this is going to give me some nightmares.

Aiden paces back and forth in the tiny room as he tells me the story. "Remember the first time we ran into each other at the hotel slightly over a month ago?" I nod. "You took a picture of your client's husband in the hotel room." I nod again, although he isn't looking at me for confirmation. "You also took a picture of something you shouldn't have."

I search my mind. What the hell did I inadvertently take a picture of? I come up with a blank. "I don't think so. I only took a picture of the couple. Nothing more."

"It seems Mr. Jessup was hiding in the bathroom of the motel room."

My eyes widen. "He was? But if he was hiding, I didn't get his picture." Furthermore, I deleted pictures from that day after Jones visited me at the office.

"Jessup needed to be sure."

"But why was he there? This doesn't make any sense."

"The woman your husband's client was having an affair with? She later disappeared."

"What?" My eyes practically jump out of my head. "Did Jessup disappear her?" Wait. Is 'disappear her' a thing?

Aiden shrugs. "We can't prove it, but all the evidence points to him."

"I totally want my fifty bucks back from Ralph. He should have never let the other guy in the room. Or at least he should have told me."

Aiden growls. "Do not make light of this situation. You were in danger. I should have never left you alone in your house."

"You are not my keeper. Besides, it was fine. Lola was there and the security system alerted the police who arrived in minutes." Lola lifts her head and barks upon hearing her name.

He grunts. "Not good enough. I should have never left the woman I love alone when I knew there was a possibility she was in danger."

"Whoa. Wait a minute." I hold up my hands and back away. "The woman you love? You don't know me well enough."

He chuckles. "Honey, I've known you practically my entire life." He shrugs. "Besides, when you know, you know." I can't argue with him there. "And I know you love me."

"How can you possibly know how I'm feeling?" It's true. But I only admitted it to myself when I was hiding in the bathroom scared out of my freaking mind.

He smirks and stalks after me. I back up until I'm pinned against the wall. "You nearly told me the other night when we had the picnic."

Oh crap. I cringe. "You noticed, huh?"

He bends forward and rubs his nose against mine. I do not sigh. Seriously. It was a cough or something. "I'm a detective. I notice everything about you."

"This does not bode well for my future."

"Honey." He pulls me into his arms. "This bodes extremely well for your future and you know it."

His head descends and then his lips are on mine. His taste of sunshine and summer is like a drug and I want more. I tilt my head to deepen the kiss. He laces his hands through my hair, and I sink my nails into his shoulders. He growls before ending the kiss and pulling back.

I pout. "Why are you stopping?" Never mind we're in a police station. No one can see us. I'm sure this room has seen way worse things than a couple making out anyway. Ew. Maybe we should go home.

Aiden places his forehead against mine. "I want to hear the words."

"The words," I immediately quip.

"Smart ass. You know what I want to hear."

I keep my mouth firmly shut. I'm not ready to say the words he wants to hear. I admitted my feelings to myself for the first time tonight for gosh sakes. I need time to process.

"Come on," he coaxes. "Tell me what I want to hear, and I'll take you home and do you dirty all night long."

I snort. "The night is almost over."

"You are a pain in my ass."

And damn proud of it, too.

"Please, Hailey, honey. I love you. I want to hear you say you love me, too. I promise I won't abuse your love and I'll spend the rest of my life proving myself worthy of your love."

I raise an eyebrow. "Promise. Like forever and ever?"

"Yep."

Lola woofs, obviously not happy with being left out of the forever scenario. Aiden rolls his eyes and looks down at her. "You, too. I'll give you lots of puppy treats and take you on long walks." He scratches her behind the ear until her tongue lolls out of her mouth.

Once the dog is completely satisfied, which is super easy to do since she's a bit of an ear-scratch-slut if you want to know the truth, Aiden focuses his attention on me. "What is it going to be? Are you going to admit what we both know? Or are you going to stand there and be a chicken shit?"

I glare at him. I am not a chicken shit. I'm merely cautious. The only man I've ever told I love you to is Pops. This is a big deal. He bawks and my glare intensifies. "Fine. I love you. Are you happy now?"

"Ecstatic," he murmurs before his lips descend and mold to mine. Before I get a chance to pull him close and devour his mouth, he pulls away.

I throw my arms in the air. "What now?"

"Now, I take you home and make good on my promise."

My eyes round and my body heats. "Oh."

"Yeah, oh. Close your mouth, honey."

Damn. I might be drooling.

Chapter 34

How is sex like a game of bridge? If you have a great hand, you don't need a partner. ~ Text from Hailey to Aiden

AIDEN STOPS BEFORE WE can enter McGraw's Pub. "What's wrong?"

I consider lying to him for approximately zero point five seconds, but I've learned in the past week since we both said *I love you*, the man is not to be tricked. Nope. He notices everything. I haven't made up my mind yet on whether it's endearing or annoying as shit.

"I'm nervous," I admit.

He yanks on my hand and pulls me near. "Why?"

I shrug. "Never mind. I'm being an idiot." I start to walk in the pub, but he doesn't let me move an inch.

"Nice try. Try again."

"Fine." I huff. Him noticing everything is definitely in the annoying as shit column right now. "I've never walked into Pops' bar with a boyfriend before." He smirks and I start backpedaling. "Not like I haven't had a boyfriend before, but never one he's approved of."

His smirk grows. "Good," he says before kissing my forehead. "Now, let's go. I need a drink after the week I've had."

"The week you've had?" Snort. "You have no idea. I've spent the week listening to Suzie bounce off the walls while shouting, I told you so." The only reprieve I got is when she bounced straight into a wall and knocked herself out. Seriously. Knocked herself clean out.

I open the door and shout, "Honey, I'm home!"

The uncles are gathered around the bar gabbing to Pops. Yes, gabbing. If you think old men don't gab, you are wrong. Very, very wrong. They gab more than old women. I look around but Suzie and Phoebe haven't arrived yet.

"Hey, Pops." I walk behind the bar and give the old man a hug. "How are you?"

"How are you coping?" he asks in response. Pops has turned into a worrywart since the break-in. Talk about suffocating. If it weren't for Aiden, he probably would have shipped me off to a nunnery by now and we're not even Catholic.

"I'm fine." And I am fine. Sure, I may have had some nightmares, but Aiden has been with me the entire time. Between him and Lola, I couldn't be safer.

Pops looks across the bar at Aiden for confirmation. Fortunately for Aiden, he nods. I shake my head. Men. I join Aiden on the other side of the bar. He wraps his arm around me and pulls me close.

"Hey, Hailey. What kind of bees produce milk?" Barney asks. "Boobees," he answers his own joke while laughing. He raises a hand for a high-five, but I don't move.

"Lame," I tell him.

Lenny and Wally bend over to kiss my cheek before giving Aiden chin lifts.

"Hey, Hails." Sid greets me with a kiss on the forehead. "One down, two to go."

"Two to go what?" Suzie asks as she joins us with Phoebe in tow.

I shake my head at Sid, but he pays me no mind. "Two left to find men."

She looks around. "Who?" When everyone looks at her, she points to herself. "Me?" She guffaws. "Um, no. No men for me. Now her?" She points to Phoebe. "We can totally hook her up."

Phoebe's face turns a bright shade of red. "Um, no thanks?"

I slap Sid on the arm. "You've got your work cut out for you." I look around and notice our group is complete. All the uncles are here as well as Suzie and Phoebe. "Come on, let's grab our table."

Suzie and Phoebe start to walk to the table, but the uncles don't move. Uh oh. They're up to no good again. I elbow Lenny, but he shakes his head. Guess we're going to wait and see.

"Babycakes, can you cover for me? Need to hit the head."

I move around the bar to play bartender. I grab a mug and set it under the tap to pour a beer. When I look up, the uncles aren't watching me. No, their attention is riveted to the end of the hallway where the restrooms are.

I put the mug down and cross my arms over my chest. "What did you do?"

"Nothing," Barney says. The devious smile on his face says something else entirely.

I sigh and rest my hip against the counter and wait. It doesn't take long. There's a shout from the restroom before Pops comes rushing down the hallway. His face is red and there's sweat on his brow.

"Can you cover for me, Hailey? I need to go to the hospital."

He opens the drawer to grab his wallet. When he turns around and notices the uncles, he freezes. The uncles aren't giving anything away, but Pops knows them too well. He slams the drawer shut. "You fuckers. What did you put in my coke?"

Barney bends over laughing while Sid and Lenny shrug as if they have no clue what he's talking about. The smirks on their faces make liars of them.

"You should have never messed with my burger," Wally announces and then does an about-face and walks to our table.

Pops stares at Wally's retreating figure, and I can see the wheels spinning in his head already.

"Let's get this party started," Suzie shouts as she skips to the table. She doesn't look where she's going. Of course not. Why would she start now? She runs into a table, bounces off it, and lands on a customer's lap.

"Well, hello, beautiful. Nice of you to drop in," the man says with a wink.

Suzie screams and her legs pedal in the air. Aiden takes pity on her and walks over to help her up. "Come on, klutzy girl."

"I'm not a klutz!" she shouts as she smooths down her top.

"I don't mind klutzy," the man she landed on announces.

"Don't encourage her, Carl," Pops shouts from behind the bar.

"But she's cute," he whines.

"And not interested in a beer-swilling barfly."

Suzie stops and walks back to him. "What kind of beer do you prefer? Are there flavors you don't like? Do you prefer an APA over an IPA?" She machine-guns questions at him.

I grab her hand. "Excuse us, Carl."

"No problem, Babycakes."

Aiden growls and pulls me behind him to face down Carl. "You don't call her Babycakes."

I move in front of him and use both hands to push his chest. He doesn't budge, so I do it again. "You don't get to decide who calls me Babycakes or not. I might find it sexy when you get all possessive in the bedroom, but possessive behavior needs to stay in the bedroom. You hear me?" I push him once again in case he didn't get the drift.

Pops growls. "Too much information!"

Suzie shushes him. "You hush. I want all the deets."

My face heats as I realize what I said. Aiden chuckles and throws an arm around me. "Message received," he says before nuzzling my neck. "I like it when you get all growly," he whispers.

"Get your asses over here, lovebirds. I'm starving," Wally shouts and my stomach rumbles.

Aiden chuckles. "Are you sure Wally's not your real father?"

I elbow him in the stomach before joining the others at the table. Pops walks over to take our orders. "A round of burger and fries." He looks at Phoebe. "And what would you like, darling?"

Phoebe bites her lip. "Can I try a burger?"

I look at Suzie who widens her eyes. "Our baby girl is growing up," she says with a hand over her heart.

I slap her hand. "Stop it. Don't embarrass Phoebe."

Phoebe clears her throat and straightens her back. "It's okay. I can take it."

"Good for you, girl," Lenny says and nods in approval. Phoebe ducks her head to hide her blush. I don't want to ruin her moment, but she does not want Lenny's approval. His approval comes coupled with a stifling overprotectiveness. She'll learn.

Pops arrives with a huge tray of burgers and fries. My stomach growls again. When Aiden smirks, I elbow him. "I can't help it I'm hungry all the time."

Pops catches my eye as he sets the salt shaker on the table. He doesn't need to say a word. Okay, then. Looks like the pranks are continuing today. Yippee. Not.

Wally grabs his plate close and pulls the bun of the burger to make sure it's actual meat. He smiles when he sees the pickle and onions. He grabs the salt shaker.

"Salt isn't good for you, Wally," I say knowing it will only spur him on to use more salt. What can I say? I am my father's daughter after all.

Wally shakes but no salt comes out of the shaker. He grunts and shakes harder. I lean away from the danger zone. The top pops off and a shower of foam drenches his burger. From experience, I know his burger is now drenched in lemon juice and baking soda. He pushes his burger away and stands.

"I'm sorry, Hailey, but I'm going to kill your father," he growls and storms off.

I shrug my shoulders and dive into my burger.

"You don't seem concerned," Aiden notices.

"This…" I motion to the mess on the table. "…is what I grew up with."

A busboy arrives to clean the table while we all dig into our food. I groan as I take big bites of my burger. Aiden comes close and whispers in my ear, "If you don't stop groaning, I'm going to take you into the restroom and have my wicked way with you."

"What's stopping you?" I tease before taking another bite and groaning obnoxiously loud.

He moans in response before grabbing my hand and placing it over the front of his jeans. I smirk before squeezing his cock.

Phoebe stands. "I'm…uh…" She points to the hallway leading to the restrooms.

I stand. "I'll go with you."

"I'm fine."

I shrug. "Okay," I say and sit back down.

Suzie rubs her hands together. "This is going to be good."

"What are you talking about now, crazy pants?"

She points to a man at the end of the bar. A mountain of a man whose eyes are glued to Phoebe as she walks past him on her way to the restroom. We watch to make sure he doesn't follow her. He doesn't move, but his eyes remain trained on the hallway.

"How is it you can be observant when it comes to people, but you can't watch where you're walking?" Aiden asks.

The uncles chuckle, but Suzie is unaffected by their teasing. "I watch where I walk. I can't help it people keep putting things in my way."

Aiden looks at me. "Is she serious?"

I shrug. Who knows when it comes to her?

"She's back."

I return my attention to the hallway to see Phoebe come walking out. The big, burly man stands and approaches her. Her eyes widen to saucers. I start to stand. Someone needs to rescue her. Aiden stops me. "Give her a chance."

I frown but don't move. I stand there, ready to pounce on any man who gives my girl a hard time. I don't care how big and scary he looks.

The man bends over and speaks to Phoebe. Her eyes widen further as she shakes her head. Then, she squeaks and runs away from him toward our table. She arrives with her chest heaving.

Interesting. My curiosity is officially piqued.

"Is it time to go home yet?" Aiden asks.

I wrinkle my nose at him. It's Friday night and barely past eight. I planned to stay for a few more hours. He grabs my hand and places it over the front of his jeans again. Looks like a change of plans is in order.

"Yep! Time to go home."

Chapter 35

Darcy to Elizabeth I'm sorry I roasted you, I was trying to flirt~ Text from Aiden to Hailey

I RE-READ THE TEXT from Aiden. Is he making a Jane Austen joke? In the months since we've been together, I may have forced him to watch movie interpretations of *Pride and Prejudice* and *Sense and Sensibility* a time or two. If this is the result, I'll be forcing him to read the novels next.

I giggle. Yeah, right. My six-foot-three-inch detective boyfriend wouldn't be caught dead reading Jane Austen. I rub my hands together. This is exactly why e-readers were invented. That's Aiden's birthday present all wrapped up. Awesome.

I pull open the door to McGraw's Pub with a smile on my face. The smile freezes when I get a look at the interior. What in the world? This is not the bar I know and love. There's now a makeshift stage against the far wall with a curtain in front of it and all the tables have disappeared to be replaced by rows of chairs.

Am I in the wrong place? I look at the bar and there stands Aiden. "Where's Pops? What's going on?"

"It's a surprise."

I pop my hip out and place a hand on it. "When have I ever given you the impression I like surprises?"

He smirks. "Whenever I wake you up with my—"

"Finish that sentence at your peril, young man," my father shouts from the kitchen.

I giggle as I walk to the bar. "What are you up to?"

"Remember when we first met."

"Yes, I was a freshman and—" He stops me before I have a chance to tell the horribly embarrassing story of how I lost the ability to speak the first time I saw him.

"No. When we met again a few months ago and you accused me of not recognizing you."

"Duh. You didn't recognize me."

He smirks. "On our first date, I promised to prove to you I wasn't the asshole in high school you thought I was."

I walk to him and fish the dog tag I gave him out of his shirt and fiddle with it. "Yeah, you showed me this and told me you wore it the entire time you were deployed."

"This is very romantic. I should take notes," Sid says from wherever he's hidden.

Aiden lowers his voice. "There's more to the story." I cock an eyebrow and wait. "I attended every play you were in while in high school."

"You did?" I wrinkle my brow as I try to imagine the most popular guy in high school going to one of my plays. "But I never saw you."

"Nevertheless, I was there."

"Darn. I wish I had known." Although, I probably would have been completely tongue-tied and ruined the play had I known.

"Do you remember the last play you performed in high school?"

I don't have to think about it. "*Pride and Prejudice*. Classic Jane Austen."

Aiden sweeps his arm out. "Welcome to Netherfield."

I look around the bar. There's no indication we're in 19th Century Nottinghamshire England. "I'm not seeing it."

Pops walks out of the kitchen dressed in Regency era formal wear. He pulls at his collar while muttering curses under his breath.

"I've humped a sixty while wearing a flak vest and let me tell you, young woman, it was more comfortable than this garb," he grumbles.

I have no idea what he's talking about, but I nod as if I commiserate.

"Mr. Bennet, I presume." I curtsy.

"What happens now?" I ask.

Aiden pushes me toward the office. "Now, you get changed for your performance."

"We're going to perform *Pride and Prejudice*? But I haven't studied my lines."

Aiden winks. "You'll be fine. I believe in you."

I open the door to the office to find Suzie and Phoebe waiting for me. They're both wearing dresses typical of the Austen era. Bare necks and low necklines with short puffy sleeves, and long skirts embellished with lace. Suzie is holding a dress up for me. "Time to shine, drama geek."

I quickly strip before putting the dress on. "At least we don't have to wear bodiced petticoats and silk stockings and slippers."

"Wouldn't a bodiced petticoat help to create a bit of cleavage?" Suzie asks.

I glare at her before addressing Phoebe. "I'm not sure if I should be proud of her for knowing what a bodiced petticoat is or mad at her for pointing out my lack of bosom."

Phoebe doesn't answer me as she hands me a pair of ballerina slippers. "Put these on. I'll do your hair."

"Can anyone tell me what is going on?"

"Just go with it," Suzie says as Phoebe brushes my hair.

Within five minutes I'm dressed like a stand-in for a Jane Austen movie with my hair in a typical Regency hairstyle. I'm breathing hard as if I've run a marathon. I wave my hands under my armpits to stop the nervous sweat trying to break free. "What now?"

Suzie pushes me toward the door. "Now, you act."

I studied drama. I should be excited to be on stage. Spoiler alert – I'm not. Not when I haven't studied my lines, and everyone is acting cuckoo for cocoa puffs.

Aiden is waiting for me at the end of the hallway. He's changed into Regency era clothing as well. And he makes it look good. Way better than in any of those *Pride and Prejudice* movie remakes I've watched. And I've watched them all. Eat your heart out Colin Firth.

He holds out his arm. "Shall we?"

What the hell. I walk to him and place my hand in the crook of his elbow. We stroll into the bar and step onto the stage. I look around. The place is no longer empty. The chairs are now filled with all our friends and family.

"Are we seriously performing *Pride and Prejudice* for them? Did you memorize your lines?"

Aiden winks. "You'll see," he whispers before raising his head and calling out, "Lights!"

Everyone falls silent as the lights dim and a spotlight shines on us. "Thank you, everyone, for coming out tonight." He waits until the clapping dies down before beginning again. "As you know, my Hailey loves to act and is obsessed with Jane Austen."

"I wouldn't say obsessed."

"Totally obsessed," Suzie yells out from somewhere in the back of the room.

"Anyway." Aiden clears his throat. "I thought a play would be the perfect way to show her I'm here to stay."

"And embarrass her father," Pops yells out.

"What is this? Comedy hour?" I ask out of the corner of my mouth.

Aiden grabs my hands. "We're going to do the final scene."

"The prologue with an overview of the marriages of the three daughters? Am I Mrs. Bennet?"

He freezes for a moment before pointing to the corner. "Go over there."

I walk to the corner of the stage. I'm confused. The final scene of the book is boring. Why aren't we starting at the beginning with the sparring between the parents? I shrug. Apparently, this is Aiden's show.

Aiden motions to me to walk toward him. I only just walked away but whatever. "My dear Hailey—"

"Am I not Mrs. Bennett? I don't think her first name was Hailey." I know it wasn't, but maybe he doesn't.

"This isn't working," he mumbles before dropping to one knee. "Hailey. Not Mrs. Bennett. Not Elizabeth or any of the other sisters who constantly natter away."

I giggle. Guess Aiden doesn't like the Bennett sisters much.

"I am trying to make a grand gesture to show you how much I love you."

"Good job. I'm convinced." And I am. Although I have had a few moments of panic in the past months since we've been dating, I am learning to trust in Aiden. Trust he won't run off without a word. Pops also set me aside and explained some things about my mother, which helped a lot. But that's a story for another time.

Aiden smiles and reaches into his pocket. He pulls out a small black box. He holds it in front of him and pops it open. I gasp and cover my face with my hands. Is this really happening? I peek between my fingers. Yep, this is happening. Inside the box is a diamond engagement ring. And it is gorgeous – a round diamond mounted on a band of white gold.

He grabs my hand. "Hailey McGraw, will you continue to annoy me by making me watch Jane Austen films for the rest of my life?"

I stomp my foot, which has no effect considering I'm wearing ballerina slippers. "It was two movies!"

"I love you, Hailey. Say you'll be my wife."

I smile at him. "As if I could ever say no to you."

"I'm not hearing a yes."

I roll my eyes. "Yes, Aiden Barnes I will be your wife."

He springs to his feet, but I hold out a hand. "But I have conditions."

"Always with the conditions!" Suzie shouts.

I ignore her. "You will accept I am an independent woman and won't try to boss me around."

"Except in the bedroom."

Pops groans. "We didn't need to hear that!"

Aiden smirks and pulls me into his arms to twirl me around. "She said yes!"

"We heard!" Uncle Sid shouts back.

I slap him on the shoulder. "Put me down. I want to see my ring."

"Such a girl."

I don't bother to respond. I grab the box from him and pull out the ring. I shove it on my finger and stick my hand out to admire it. "You done good, boy."

Pops ambles onto the stage. "What do I always tell you, Babycakes? Love will out."

"It sure will," I say and throw my arms around him.

"Hey." Aiden pushes us apart. "I'm the one she's supposed to be hugging."

"Young man, you have her for the rest of your life. I'm the one saying goodbye."

My eyes tear up. "You are not saying goodbye to a daughter. You're saying hello to a son."

Pops nods. "I approve."

I throw my head back and laugh because life is good. Not only have I found the love of my life, but Pops likes him. Nothing could ruin this day. Nothing.

D.E. Haggerty

Love and Laughter in Every Chapter

About the Author

D.E. Haggerty is an American who has spent the majority of her adult life abroad. She has lived in Istanbul, various places throughout Germany, and currently finds herself in The Hague. She has been a military policewoman, a lawyer, a B&B owner/operator and now a writer.